WAGON WHEEL GAP

ALSO BY B.N. RUNDELL

WAGON WHEEL GAP

A QUEST CHRONICLES NOVEL
BOOK 7

B.N. RUNDELL

WOLFPACK
PUBLISHING
— EST 2013 —

Wagon Wheel Gap
Paperback Edition
Copyright © 2025 by B.N. Rundell

Wolfpack Publishing
1707 E. Diana Street
Tampa, FL 33610

www.wolfpackpublishing.com

Editing by My Brother's Editor

Paperback ISBN 979-8-89567-787-2
Ebook ISBN 979-8-89567-786-5
LCCN 2025947118

Time is getting short, I turned 80 this last year and I'm feeling it in my old bones! So, as my writing career, like my time on earth, is getting shorter, I'd like to dedicate this novel to the many faithful readers that have read every book! I've heard from many that started reading almost as soon as I started writing, and most (not all!) have been blessed by the books and the many characters. On occasion, I have used the names (with permission) of some of these readers as characters, and even built the characters after their real life. One, a special friend, even asked to be a character that had been captured by the natives and given an Indian name! That was Coyote Howling! But it's all been fun and a great adventure. So... I dedicate this book to the adventuresome many that have traveled these historical roads with me. Thanks for the ride!

WAGON WHEEL GAP

1

TRAVELING

THE SHADOWS STRETCHED LONG BEFORE HIM, SLOWLY fading as the grey light of early morning brushed the brighter colors of sunrise from the sky. The silhouetted sawtooth eastern horizon had been replaced by the rocky slopes of the La Garita mountain range that caught and held the rising sunlight with rocky crags and snow-filled crevasses. Cordell Beckett stretched his lanky frame and pushed back the brim of his dusty black, flat-brimmed hat, slapped some pale-brown dust from his long duster, and breathed deep of the crisp mountain air. He straddled the long-legged grulla stallion he aptly named Kwitcher. While Cord was still a youth and training the horse, he often called out, "Kwit cher stompin'. Kwit cher tossin' your head!" and the name stuck. The frisky Kwitcher was a crossbreed of Morgan and Mustang and was a smart, quick responding, and fast-stepping stallion. Trailing behind was the pack mule that had been following Kwitcher all the miles they traveled together. Beside Cord loped the flop-eared hound called Blue, best friends and traveling companions for many years.

Tucked inside the lower vest pocket of Cord was a US Marshal badge given him by the Territorial Marshal Sheffenberg when Cord had asked for some authority to seek out and find the killers of his family —all outlaw members of the Civil War Red Legs. It was a task he had recently completed, and the marshal asked for Cord to continue as the marshal for the third district of the territory of Colorado, a district that encompassed the southwest quarter of what would one day become the state of Colorado. It was a district that was mostly unpopulated with the few residents being either gold prospectors or outlaws. Problems had begun to run unchecked with no lawmen of any kind in the area, although the valley of the Rio Grande had a few early settlers that came in the time of the Spaniard settlements when the Mexican government was trying to settle the land as a greater claim for the territory. Now, the task of bringing the law to this part of the territory had fallen to Cord, and he was headed to the heart of the district, howbeit somewhat reluctantly, to fulfill the promise to the marshal.

Cord was confident in his position, always properly armed with his Winchester Yellow Boy rifle in .44 caliber, his Remington Army pistol in .44 caliber, converted to metal cartridges, and his Greener shotgun. He had included extra ammunition for all his weapons, even the seldom-used Spencer .56 caliber rifle with the telescopic sights. He was more than competent in the use of all his weapons, having been taught from a young age by his father. His father, who had served as the pastor of their local church, had fought with the British during the Battle of Pinjarra and had received an officer's commission. He also fought with the Ottoman Empire as an officer during the revolt in Tripolitania. Although his father would never talk about his wartime exploits, he shared with Cord the many ways of fighting he learned. What had suited Cord the best was the hand-to-hand combat, or what would become known as martial arts. What he learned from his father was a unique blend of Muay Thai and Capoeira with elements of jiu-jitsu. But Cord had developed his own style using moves from all those taught by his father, for his father always said, "You have to use what is natural and comfortable for you, not what works for others. Sometimes you may have to defend your life, or the lives of others, and you won't always have a weapon other than your own body."

Cord remembered the many times he and his father sat in the woods, rifles across their laps, hunting for meat for the family, but spending the time learning and sharing. Moments that stayed with Cord for all his life and that he would often draw from as the situation called for experience beyond his own.

The Rio Grande River meandered its way east from the higher mountains of the San Juans and the La Garita range. The waters caught the early morning sun and bounced the lances of light back toward Cord, bringing his attention to the present. He found himself often letting his thoughts turn to his past and the time spent with Lone Eagle, the *Puwagat* or medicine woman of the Ute people. And before that, his wife of two years, who had died in childbirth as she had the child. His thoughts also brought forth the memory of Yellow Singing Bird, a young woman he helped return to her people, but who also gave her life in a fight with Cord's early confrontation with the Red Leg outlaws. He had since determined he would ride the trail alone and fulfill his promise to Marshal Sheffenberg to bring law to the southwest corner of Colorado Territory, but that did not keep his heart and mind from the trail of reminiscing.

As the flat lands of the San Luis Valley receded, they gave way to the foothills that crowded their way closer to the Rio Grande River, the river that had been called the River Del Norte by the early settlers. Now the valley showed evidence of some of the early settlers that had abandoned their homesteads in years gone by, but there were several that still stood. Fields had been cleared and crops planted, irrigation ditches carved into the hard clay soil, and green was showing in the fields. One man stood behind the plow he was hitching to a team of mules and waved at the passing Cord, who nodded and returned the wave. Cord grinned and remembered his own time on their small farm in Missouri when his father taught him to harness the mules and hitch the plow and make a straight furrow. He shook his head at what he knew then and now remembered that his father thought it was useless to try to make Cord into a farmer. Always a reader of books and with a wandering mind, he was determined to explore and seek adventure. But little did he know how God was preparing him for what was to come.

The trail he traveled kept to the south of the river, away from the thicker undergrowth and clusters of cottonwoods and alders that sided the river. The land before him was dry land country showing some gramma grasses, lots of cacti, both hedgehog and prickly pear, with many clumps of yucca, cholla, and sage brush in abundance. The grey-green of the sage coloring the entire land and sliding up the lower flanks of the foothills, giving way to the darker greens of piñon and twisted cedar of the lower foothills. It was a dry country, and every footfall of the horse brought puffs of dust that filtered its way up the dark legs of the grulla and covered the trousers and boots of Cord. He felt the warmth of the rising sun on his back and lifted his hat to wipe the sweat from his brow and neck. Looking ahead, he saw a break in the trees at the river's edge and decided a short break and some fresh water for himself and the animals would be appreciated.

A group of three mule deer were on the far side of the river, noses in the water, but eyes across the stream. When Cord came from the trees, the three bucks, all with antlers in the velvet, lifted their heads and quickly scampered away. Cord grinned as he stepped to the ground and led the big grulla to the water, where Blue was already drinking while his ears floated on the clear backwater. Cord dropped the reins and Kwitcher lowered his nose for a deep drink as Cord waited. When the animals' thirst was sated, Cord doffed his hat, dropped to one knee, and with a cupped hand, lifted water for drink, his eyes and ears always watchful.

His first sip was refreshing but not quenching, and he dropped his hand for another, unconsciously dropping his head and shoulders in the movement. As he dipped his hand in the cold water, a shrill whistling passed his shoulder, startling the horse, the pack mule, Blue, and causing all to jolt to the side. Cord dropped to his belly, his arm in the water, but he rolled to his back and brought his Colt to his hand as he looked back through the brush toward the open valley. Nothing stirred as the boom of the gunshot racketed across the valley, bouncing from rocky cliff to stone abutment as it echoed its way across the stillness. A slow soaring eagle high overhead screamed his alarm, as a small flock of grosbeaks fluttered from the cottonwoods nearby.

But all was still, and it seemed even the leaves of the aspen and cottonwoods had ceased to move in the mountain breeze. Nothing stirred. Cord crawled on his belly to the edge of the trees, peering out from under the thick alders, watching the valley bottom with its clusters of sage, and still nothing moved. He was not certain where the shot came from, but he thought it was from the valley behind him or the foothills beyond. Although it would be a long shot from the foothills, he guessed the distance to be near five hundred yards, but that was not impossible. He remembered the unusual sound of the bullet, and he remembered his father talking about a sniper rifle used by the Confederacy called a Whitworth sniper rifle and how its bullets made a shrill whistle as they spun through the air. It had something to do with the rifling of the barrel and the shape of the bullet, and the weapon was well known for long range, even up to 2000 yards, accuracy.

Cord shook his head at the thought of a sniper's bullet coming that close, but he was also concerned about who would know he was coming and would be out to stop him. Or was it just a mistake or maybe a wanton killer out to kill anyone, even a stranger? Cord was in no hurry to find out and waited for any movement that might give away his wannabe assailant, but nothing stirred. But Cord was smart enough to know that an experienced sniper had patience and would wait for his target to be the first to move and consequently die. He breathed deep, and slowly began to pull back, inching through the thickets of alder and kinnikinnick, getting snagged by thorns occasionally, but stealthily moving into the thicker brush and trees where the animals had drawn and now lazily grazed on the tall grasses at river's edge.

It was coming on late morning, and he had far to go, but until he found either the shooter or evidence of his leaving, he could not risk exposing himself. When he reached the clearing with the animals, he rose beside Kwitcher and slipped the Spencer with its telescopic sight from the scabbard and checked the load. Satisfied, he looked at the river, stepped aboard the grulla and nudged the big horse to the water, with the mule's lead wrapped around the saddle horn, the rifle across his lap, and Blue eagerly taking to the water. The current of white water splashed against Cord's leg, rising almost to his knee as Kwitcher fought the current but quickly made the crossing. Once on the far side and in the trees, Cord stepped down and looked across the river, but saw they were well covered with the thick cottonwoods and alders. Satisfied, he turned and started up the steep piñon-covered slope, his eye on the rocky outcropping of a shoulder higher up. That would give him a good vantage point to scan the valley and hopefully spot the shooter before being seen.

2

HUNT

CORD WAS AT HOME IN THE HIGH COUNTRY OF THE Rockies. Many a time, he had to stalk prey for food and even more often stalk an enemy, whether a native or an outlaw. He moved easily over the rocky hillside, his choice of route, winding through the thicker clusters of piñon and twisted cedar. But as he neared the rocky outcroppings, he had to carefully make his way over the loose rock that could easily move under his weight and give away his location. Now on all fours with his rifle slung over his back, he moved from one outcropping to another and finally found the notch he spotted from below and slipped over the crest of the rocks, belly down in the pine needles, and began his search of the hillside beyond for any sign of his would-be assailant.

He used the cover of an overhanging branch to prevent any glare from his binoculars and slowly scanned the entire face of the hills. Nothing moved, no dust, not even a pine cone dropping. He saw a black and white magpie take flight, but it wasn't a sudden move. The bird slowly circled overhead and watched the terrain below. He wasn't frightened, just hungry. Cord waited and watched, spotting what he thought was a possible location where the shooter had been. A bit of disturbed soil and pine needles at the base of a big rock that could have been used as a rest for the shooter. He scanned closer, spotted what might have been where a horse had been tethered, and nothing more.

Cord was certain the shooter had already gone, but he waited a few more moments, then began his descent, still careful not to give himself away in case the shooter had only moved to a different vantage point and was waiting for Cord to expose himself. When he neared the edge of the river, he mounted up and turned upstream, staying covered in the trees for a good mile before crossing back to the thicker cottonwoods and alders. He stepped down and scanned the countryside before mounting up and returning to the trail.

He was a little mystified about the shooter. Cord believed no one knew he was coming nor did they know he was a deputy marshal. He had never been one to brazenly display the badge and dare anyone to use it as a target, although he knew some lawmen that were prone to strut their authority, it was not his way.

The trail turned more west as it skirted the river, and as the sun was lowering beyond, Cord saw a few buildings at the mouth of a long canyon that split the mountains on the north of the valley. He knew this would be South Fork, so named because of the confluence of the South Fork of the Rio Grande and the headwaters of the Rio Grande rivers. It wasn't much of a settlement, with two sod roofed log cabins, one larger building with a crude sign stating it was a trading post and hotel, but differed little from the soddies. As Cord looked around, he knew this had been the land of the Muache or Uncompahgre Ute under Chief Ouray, but the treaty had long been broken, and they were negotiating a new one.

Two horses and a mule stood hipshot at the hitchrail before the trading post, while a separate hitchrail at the side stood lonely. Cord nudged Kwitcher to the side and stepped to the ground, slapped Kwitcher's reins and the lead of the pack mule over the hitchrail, and after a once-over of the tack, especially the rifle scabbards on the horses and mule before the building, and satisfied, he stepped to the open door. He ducked into the dim interior and was greeted by a "Howdy friend!" from an aproned man that stood behind what he considered to be a counter, which was nothing more than a couple of boards across the space between two barrels. The pot-bellied man had long handle-bar moustache drooping past his chin, and what appeared to be his breakfast on his apron as he leaned on the counter, grinning and glancing to the two men that sat at a barrel with drinks in their hands as they were shadowed by the dim sun light that struggled to pierce the speckled window behind them.

Cord nodded, "Howdy," and stepped close to the counter.

"Ain't seen you 'round'chere afore," declared the clerk, expecting an answer.

"Nope," answered Cord, then motioned to the others, "What're they drinkin'?"

"Rotgut, or whiskey if you wanna call it that. I don't make it, but a feller o'er the hill yonder," nodding behind his building, "Makes it so he can keep diggin' fer gold."

"How 'bout coffee? Got'ny?"

"It's pro'ly stronger'n the whiskey, but I got some," he declared, as he turned around to step to the stove in the corner. He poured some black brew in a tin cup and sat it before Cord.

Cord grinned, lifted the cup and sipped at the hot brew, shook his head and said, "That'll put hair on your chest!"

"Or burn it off!" cackled one of the men at the table as he lifted his cup of whiskey. "This hyar's a man's drink!"

Cord looked at the trader and asked, "How's the trail up the river?"

"Ain't much of a trail, but the stage comp'ny had a feller through here a while back lookin' it o'er, case they wanna bring a stage line through hyar. Barlow'n Sanderson man he was."

"What kind of settlements are up thataway?" asked Cord, sipping his coffee.

"Wal, ain't much 'cepin' some miners huntin' gold. Some have found a little color, but ain't much. Injuns still come thru hyar and scare most of 'em off. But there's a couple cabins at the mouth of the canyon. I think they's callin' it Wagon Wheel Gap!" He laughed, "It's cuz there was a feller tried to bring a wagon 'crost the river and lost a wheel 'fore he lost his wagon. The wheel ended up on a rock in the middle an' they been callin' it Wagon Wheel Gap! Hehehehe. An' the wheel's still there!" he slapped the counter at what he thought was the foolishness of others. "B'fore that, the Ute used to camp out thar 'round them hot springs, and there's been a couple families try'n to do some farmin' up there. Reckon some of 'ems still there." He shook his head at the thought.

He looked at Cord, leaned forward on the counter, and asked, "You a miner or a farmer?"

"Nope," answered Cord, taking another sip of the coffee.

"Then what'chu doin' goin' up thar?"

"Ain't been there b'fore," answered Cord, a stoic expression on his face.

The trader frowned, "Wal, I reckon you ain't been a lotta places. That ain't no reason. You cain't see ever'thing!"

"Not if you don't even try!" answered Cord, grinning.

"There's some mighty unfriendly types up that-away. Could get dangerous!" declared a now serious trader.

Cord chuckled, "I think I already met up with one, although he didn't stick around to introduce himself."

The trader frowned, "What'chu mean?"

"Had a fella take a shot at me back down the trail. Just missed me, and then he lit out 'fore I could find him."

"How'd you know he was shootin' at you?"

"Heard the whistle of the bullet as it passed by my head!" answered Cord.

One of the two at the table spoke up and asked as he leaned toward Cord, "Did you say whistle?"

Cord turned to face him, "That's right. I've been shot at before, but none of the bullets whistled like this one."

The two men looked at one another, mumbled something to one another, then the speaker looked back at Cord. "If you're certain it was a bullet and it was whistlin', it mighta been a feller we heard 'bout what used to be a Rebel Sniper, a sharpshooter with one o' them Whitworth rifles from the war. Ain't heard much outta him lately, thought he'd left the country, but if you heard it, musta been him."

The man dropped his eyes, shook his head, "He's a big'un. A light-skinned mulattoe. Someone said his daddy was a plantation owner 'fore the war, and was an officer in the Confederacy. But his momma was a slave girl, or so they say, and that boy is mad at the world an' 'specially the White world. They say he served for the South cuz they thought he was White, but he just done it so he could kill White officers that wore a uniform an' he din't care if it was blue or grey!"

"Why was he in this country?" asked Cord.

"Reckon he was passin' as a White, prospectin' and wantin' gold like the rest of us. But they say, he found it easier to mine the pockets of the miners 'stead o' the creeks! He done kilt several, then they said he up and high tailed it outta here, but if'n what you say is true, then he might be back!"

"He have a name?" asked Cord.

"Ain't too sure what it is...heard tell some was callin' him Oby, short for Obadiah, like in the Bible. Other'n that, dunno!" declared the man, looking at his friend beside him and back to Cord.

Cord finished his coffee, stepped to the door to look at the remains of the day, and turned back to the trader, "I might be back through here. If you hear any more about this Obadiah fella, I'd like to know."

The trader nodded, and watched as Cord left the building. The trader looked at the two men at the table and shook his head, "If Oby was shootin' at me, I'd be wantin' to hightail it outta here, and he's goin' on into them hills where he's liable to find him!"

The two men looked at one another, back to the

trader, and the previously quiet one of the two said, "Just ain't no tellin' 'bout the lack o' sense of some o' them confounded fools from the flatlands!"

The other two shook their heads and mumbled their agreement and reached for another drink.

3

MOVIN' ON

THE CONFLUENCE OF THE RIO GRANDE AND THE SOUTH Fork of the Rio Grande lay in a triangle of timber-covered hills, with the two hills that stood proudly off the banks of the Rio Grande, standing tall. The northernmost hill showed rocky shoulders of granite abutments pushing free of the spruce and piñon, while the opposite hill lay serene under a cape of timber. The river coming from the northwest, at the mouth of the canyon, was about a hundred feet wide and somewhat shallow. It meandered through a long, narrow valley that was sided on the north by tall, flat-topped buttes with broad shoulders strutting imposing rocky escarpments at the edge. The south side showed sparsely timbered rolling hills.

Cord wanted isolation for his camp for the night, but followed the wagon road from the settlement to a shallows crossing where the road took to the shoulder on the north side of the river. Cord pushed

Kwitcher across, trailing the pack mule and with Blue swimming ahead. After a brief shake on the bank, he turned to follow the two-track trail into the shadows of dusk. It was a narrow trail and hung on the steep shoulder of the high-rising buttes and no more than ten to fifteen feet above the chuckling rapids of the river. After the trail rounded a point of rocks below the steep shoulder that seemed ominously threatening with massive boulders lurking high above, the valley opened wide with a farmer's green fields on the far side of the river where a small feeder creek fell from the high country. But on the north side, dry hillsides offered little cover, yet he pushed into a timbered draw to find a campsite revealed by a small cluster of aspen that marked a freshwater spring. It looked to be a comfortable site, and Cord stepped down and quickly stripped the gear from the animals, led them to the spring for a drink, and rolled out his blankets. After a quick look around, he sat down on the blankets, leaned against the white trunk of the largest aspen, and dug out some jerky for his supper.

———

HE AWAKENED to the grey light of early morning, saw the hint of color over the crest of the hills behind him, and stood, stretched, and grabbed his rifle and Bible and climbed the slope above the aspen and found a rugged shoulder of basaltic rock and seated himself to begin his day. His marker was in the book of John at chapter eight and he picked up where he had read the day before at verse 31, *Then said Jesus to those Jews which believed on him, If ye continue in my word, then are ye my disciples indeed; and ye shall know the truth, and the truth shall make you free.* Cord smiled at the thought, remembering the many times at his father's knee when he heard his father say these same words as he instructed his son in the way of life. He remembered his dad saying, *"And if you want to be a good man, it all starts with this!"* as he held the worn leather-covered Bible before him.

Cord had always sought to follow his father's example and teaching, and especially the Words of the Bible. It wasn't always easy to find the time to spend with the Lord, but it had become a priority and habit of Cord to acknowledge his own weakness and his need for the presence of the Lord in his life. That presence had begun when he prayed and accepted Christ as his Savior in his early teen years, just before the Red Legs attacked his farm and murdered his family. There was a time he was mad at God for what happened, but as he matured, he realized how wrong he was and how God had never failed him.

He stood and stretched, looked around the valley in the pale light of the slow rising sun, glanced to the sky to see some dark clouds to the northwest, shrugged, and walked back down to his camp to begin his day. He was surprised to hear the crack of a whip and the shout of a teamster that came from around the bend on the road Cord had just traveled. But Cord quickly finished rigging the animals and started from the trees as he saw a team of eight mules pulling two wagons with a teamster walking beside, cracking his whip and occasionally yelling at the recalcitrant animals.

Cord nudged Kwitcher from the trees and started to take to the trail just ahead of the team. The handler shouted, "Whoa up, whoa you stubborn mules!" and grabbed the lines to drag them to a stop. When the mules stood somewhat still, the man turned toward Cord and said, "Wal, howdy friend! Din't 'spect to see nobody on the trail this early! You headin' upstream?"

Cord grinned, leaned forward on the pommel of his saddle, and answered, "I am. Looks like you got yourself quite a load there. Where 'bouts you goin'?"

"Wal, it ain't where I'm goin', it's where I'll be stoppin' an' I ain't quite decided that" began the whiskery-faced teamster. He wore a floppy felt hat over his thick, dark hair that showed streaks of grey, a corn-cob pipe bounced about as he spoke, and one galuse held up his sagging britches. Hobnail boots gave him a solid foundation as he waved Cord closer and motioned to a rock pile. He seated himself and waited for Cord to do the same.

"Ya see, I been up this way afore. Tried muh hand at prospectin' and when I realized I wouldn't know gold from silver from plain ol' rocks, I skedaddled and went to town fer muh woman," he nodded to the lead wagon where sitting atop the high seat was a woman in a prairie dress and bonnet, head hanging as she sat unmoving, "and to get me sumpin' that I knew a little about. I was a storekeeper 'fore I come out'chere, so I thot I'd just spend what money I had left, get rigged up and loaded up and come thisaway and make muh money off them other darned fools!"

He laughed as he relit his pipe, blew a cloud of smoke and looked at a grinning Cord and continued, "So, up thisaway are some farmers, prospectors, and no-accounts, but all of 'em need supplies an' I got me some! Let's see, there's Wagon Wheel Gap where ol' Tom Boggs, Kit Carson's brother-in-law, has him a farm and couple others do too, an' there's some prospectin' goin' on. Then there's Willow, up at the bend in the river, that's showin' some promise, got some settlers startin' to farm up there and o' course there's always them daydreamin' prospectors. Then there's San Juan City, ain't much of no city, just a couple settlers an' such, and on further up there's the beginnings of what they wanna call Lake City. Then there's Animas Forks, and three Neigold brothers think they're gonna strike it rich and start their own town. So...the way I look at it, there's more promise as a general store with supplies than what the rest of 'ems doin'. An' I don't even hafta get muh hands dirty! Heheheee!"

The man took another puff on his pipe and looked at Cord, "So, how 'bout you, sonny? What'chu gonna do? Yuh don' look like no farmer, an' you ain't showin' no prospectin' gear. You up to no good?"

Cord grinned, "No, nothin' like that. I'm just passin' through, enjoying the country and meeting folks. Although I did have one take a potshot at me, but other'n that, it's all good."

"Yup. There's always somebody takin' potshots! Whether they think you'sa trespassin', or lookin' to rob 'em or they just don' like your looks, there's some that'll shoot at anything just to give 'em somethin' to talk about!" He slowly stood, looked at Cord, "Wal, sonny, I'm gonna git to movin' so I'm thinkin' you might wanna take to the trail 'fore me. I'll be seein' you up the trail, iffen you don' get ventilated! Hehehee."

Cord stood, nodded to the teamster, and swung aboard Kwitcher and heeled him to the trail with the mule close behind. With a wave of his hand he sent Blue ahead to scout the trail, and the day's ride began. The valley between the timbered hills was just shy of a half mile wide, showing ample grasses and sage with the hillsides covered with piñon, twisted cedar, juniper, and fading to ponderosa, spruce, and other pines, most showing abutments of granite shoulders and cliffs higher up. The waters of the Rio Grande carried the life-giving abundance of snowmelt south and west to eventually empty into the Gulf of Mexico. Cord continually scanned the land before him and the shoulders of the hillsides, enjoying the smell of pine and sage and the clear air of the mountains. A glance to the sky showed gathering clouds that threatened a storm, but he was not concerned, knowing he could find shelter among the trees and draws of the hills.

Cord was in no hurry and enjoyed the leisurely pace taken by Kwitcher, with Blue running back and forth to keep them on the right trail. They had ridden a good five to six miles up the long canyon when the shoulders of the buttes and high up rocky shoulders began pushing into the bottom, crowding the river closer to the southern hills. He had not taken time for a morning meal and was beginning to feel the need for some food, so Cord nudged Kwitcher through the trees that sided the river and found a nice grassy spot in the shade of some tall ponderosa and reined up, stepped down and walked to river's edge. With a broad grin, Cord returned to the packs aboard the mule and dug into one to retrieve some fishing line and hooks and the spade.

He soon had a baited line in the water with the line on the end of a long willow branch. It was just a short while, and he had two nice-sized trout flopping on the bank, and he eagerly set about starting a fire. With the coffee pot on a rock beside the flames, the cleaned fish impaled on willow withes and suspended over the hot coals, Cord sat back to savor the moment. The cool mountain air began whistling through the pines, and he was getting a bit drowsy, but his hunger kept him awake as he anticipated the meal.

Kwitcher and the mule had been enjoying their graze on the fresh grass, and Blue lay at Cord's feet, but they all came alive in an instant. Blue jumped to his feet, hackles raised, as he lowered his head, bared his teeth in a growl, and Kwitcher and the mule tossed their heads as the mule stretched out and screamed a bray while the horse spun on his heels and took to the timber. Cord jumped to his feet, looking in the direction of the trees where Blue was staring and growling, and the shadow of the woods moved with a low rumbling growl.

Cord smelled him before he saw him and the shadow rose to his hind feet, front paws with yellowish claws longer than Cord's fingers pawed at the air, as the giant of the woods cocked his head to the side, showed teeth almost as big as his claws as he let out a roar that seemed to rattle the trees and shake the branches. Cord stumbled backward, realizing his Winchester was in the scabbard on Kwitcher, the Spencer was on the pack mule, and his only weapon was his Remington .44 that sat on his hip. Cord knew if he shot the bear with his pistol, it would do little more than make him mad. Cord spoke softly to Blue, stretched out his hand toward the dog and began to backstep toward the trees.

The big grizzly looked down at Cord, glared with fire in his eyes, drool dripping from his jaws, and let out another rock-rattling roar. Cord quick-stepped backward as he saw the bear look to the fish sizzling over the coals, and knew the bear was after his lunch.

Cord never took his eyes off the beast, but he and Blue quickly ducked into the trees. With a quick glance to where Kwitcher and the mule had disappeared, Cord motioned to Blue to find the horse, and he followed close behind. The mule was standing at the edge of the trail, looking back to the trees, and Kwitcher was close behind. Both animals were trembling but appeared to be glad to see Cord and Blue.

Cord looked back toward the camp, saw nothing of the bear, and quickly went to the mule and the pack with the Spencer. He slipped the big rifle from the scabbard, checked the load, and turned toward the trees. He did not want to kill the beast, but he would not wait for him to attack either him or the horse and mule. He stood close beside Kwitcher, watching the trees, thinking of his coffee pot and the lunch he wanted, but neither was worth the risk of life and limb.

His attention was caught when he heard the crack of a long bullwhip and the shout of the trader back down the trail. The long team of mules showed around a bend, and Cord waited for the trader to approach. Cord motioned for him to stop, and the trader trotted to the head of the team and grabbed the halter to stop the team. With a frown, the man walked toward Cord, "Whatsamatta?"

"Bear! Big Grizzly! I was cooking some trout over the fire, reckon he got a whiff and wanted it more than I did, so..." he shrugged, grinning and glancing back to the trees.

"A grizz, huh? Then we might wanna get a ways up the trail away from here. Ain't no fish gonna satisfy his appetite!" declared the trader as he turned to go back to the rear of the team. Without another word, he lay the whip out before him with a loud crack that echoed across the canyon and the mules leaned into their traces to continue up the trail. Cord moved the horse and mule to the side, watched as they moved past, looked at the woman, still hunkered on the bench seat up top, and waved as they passed.

4

DOWNPOUR

THE ROAR OF THUNDER SHOOK THE HILLS AND THE ROCKY escarpments that marked the high shoulders stood strong, as even the tall pines shook in fear of the coming storm. The rolling thunder bounced across the narrow gorge of the Rio Grande and echoed repeatedly as it traveled down the canyon, leading the storm on its winding course to change the terrain. With rocks and boulders loosened by the sudden downpour, the roar of rockslides added to the cacophony of echoes and rolling thunder.

Kwitcher had lowered his head when the downpour started, but with the rumbling from above, he tossed his head and pranced, even turning to look askance at his rider. Blue had come scampering from further up the trail, chased by the beginning rivulets of the water that already threatened to turn into cascades and walls of water. Cord dug heels to the big stallion, pointing him to the tall timber of the hillside and the dark woods that lay in the shadow of a towering granite abutment that loomed over the feeder draw. Water was already finding its course down the smaller cut, but a narrow game trail that kept to the high ground led Cord and his animals to the overhang that showed black and hinted at dry shelter.

As he neared, Cord leaned forward, holding the brim of his hat up to peer into the dark overhang and nudged Kwitcher into the cover. Once out of the downpour, Cord quickly dropped to the ground, dropped the reins to ground hitch the grulla and walked into the shadowy cavern. Satisfied, he returned to the animals and led them further under cover. It was a clamshell-looking cavern, but did not go much further under the rocks. Black showed on the roof, evidence of other campers. A stack of wood in the corner offered fuel for a campfire and Cord quickly set-to, knowing the fire would offer warmth and comfort against the raging storm. Once the fire was going, he stripped the animals of their gear, picketed them well back from the edge of the over-hang, and rolled out his own blankets. He knew it would be a while before the storm passed and the floodwaters would allow passage. The rampaging downpour did little to muffle the echoing and rack-eting thunder and explosive lightning strikes.

Hunger still gnawed at him, and he began to prepare a pot with water, jerky, and some bacon. The dented coffee pot he retrieved after the grizzly left the earlier campsite, now sat at the edge of the fire, and Cord was anxious to get some hot coffee down his gullet. He sat back, coffee in hand, with the pot of mountain man stew at his side and began his feast.

It was some time before his hunger was sated, and he began to relax. The distant roar of the river and crashing of runoff water coming from the rocky-shouldered buttes now filled the canyon. A glance to the mouth of the cavern and he realized the thunder and lightning had abated and the storm had already lessened to a steady downpour. But in the distance, he could hear the increasing roar of the rapids of the many gully washers and the heavy flow of the Rio Grande. He shook his head at the thought of the river and the waters, thought of the trader and his woman with the double wagon hook-up behind the eight-up team of mules, and hoped they had found shelter. But for now, there was nothing he could do but prepare his camp and bedroll for the coming night.

The intermittent dripping of runoff water lulled Cord to stretch and curl under his covers to seek a bit more sleep, but the crack of dawn pried open his eyelids, and he reluctantly tossed aside the blankets and sat up, his hand naturally dropping to the rifle at his side. Nothing stirred, as the horse and mule stood hipshot and heads hanging. Blue lifted his head beside Cord as his friend sat up, and he watched as Cord stood tall and stretched. Cord tossed a couple pieces of wood on the coals of last night's fire and walked to the cavern mouth to look into the valley.

The roar of the rapids from the floodwaters still filled the canyon, and Cord wondered how high the water had risen and if it covered the trail or even washed out some. But that was a concern that could wait until later, now he needed some coffee. A steady drip from the overhang offered fresh rainwater and he walked near to fill the pot. A glance at the fresh water showed it to be clear, or clear enough, and he sat the pot beside the flames of the cook fire. He grabbed his Bible and sat down to spend a little time in the Word and with his Lord in prayer, his daily habit.

The sun was peeking through the remaining clouds, trying valiantly to throw some lances of sunlight into the drenched valley, and an occasional ray of light cast shadows on the opposite hillside from the cavern's mouth. Cord stood and stepped closer, looking down the draw toward the river and could see the white water rapids carrying the runoff and making a ruckus that filled the canyon in the doing. Cord wondered about the trader and hoped he and his woman had made it safely through the storm.

He turned and started saddling Kwitcher and loading the packs on the mule, making ready to leave when he heard the echoing crack of a bullwhip from below and grinned, knowing that would be the trader. He frowned at the thought of the man trying to make it on a muddy trail with his overloaded wagons, but that was his choice, and Cord shrugged at the thought.

When Cord reached the trail, he saw the tracks of the freighter wagons and the mule teams of the trader. This was rocky country and the rocky soil shed water much easier than the forested floors of the lowlands. Although there were places where the wagon wheels dug deep, mostly it was hardrock that showed nothing but scars from shod hooves and metal-rimmed wheels.

The shoulders of the hills pushed closer to the river bottom and now the hills on the north side showed little more than steep cliffs rising above the talus slopes that held scattered juniper and piñon that clung tenaciously to the steep faces of the slopes. The trail had taken a higher route, probably because of earlier floods, but now the two-track wagon trail cut across the face of the talus slopes high above the waterline. As he rounded the shoulder of one slope, Cord caught a view of the close canyon further upstream where the river bent back to the west and southwest, rounding a point of land apparently caused by previous flood run-offs that carried the silt from the high country and dumped it at the sharp bend of the river, making a bit of an isthmus that marked the bend.

It was at that bend when Cord caught up with the trader who had stopped to give the mules a breather and for his wife to stretch her legs. They had crossed the feeder creek called Blue Creek before they stopped in the shade of some tall cottonwoods at river's edge. The trader hailed Cord and waved him close. "Howdy friend! I see you made it through that gully-washer last night. Figgered you would. Me'n Ma pulled up when it started comin' down heavy. Stretched out a tarp from the wagon, where we parked next to some trees. The mules were tethered in the trees, and we had a good windbreak so we could have a fire an' Ma put the coffee on, so we had a good night. You?"

Cord stepped down at the motion of the trader and answered, "Oh, I found a bit of a cavern up one o' them gullies, got outta the storm, fixed my supper and settled in for the night. Tweren't too bad," grinned Cord as he followed the trader back to the fire where his wife had the coffee brewing.

"Wal, we'll get into Wagon Wheel Gap 'bout mid-afternoon. Might stop there, have a looksee around to decide if'n we wanna set up shop thar," offered the trader.

Cord grinned, "By the way, my name's Cord Beckett, and I never got yours," he said as he extended his hand to shake.

The trader grinned, extended his hand and answered, "Toots! Toots Monroe, and this is muh wife, Mabel. Most folks do like I do and call her Ma, Ma Monroe."

Cord shook his hand, tipped his hat to the woman, and said, "Pleased to meet you, ma'am."

Cord looked back at Toots, "So, since you call her Ma, that mean you've got some kids?"

Toots dropped his eyes, slowly shook his head, "Did have, set o' twins, but lost 'em to Scarlet fever. They was just four," his voice dropped as he spoke and he glanced to his wife, back to Cord. "That was nigh unto six year ago, but seems like yestiddy," he mumbled as he sat on the log beside the fire. He motioned for Cord to join him and looked at him as he sat down. "Don't s'pose you had any young'uns?"

Cord shook his head, "No, but I lost my wife and baby in childbirth a couple years back."

The men hung their heads as they both leaned forward, elbows on knees, watching the woman put the coffee in the pot and move it back to the flames. Both men sat silent a moment, their minds wandering the silent halls of memories.

5

THE GAP

CORD RODE BESIDE THE WAGON AS TOOTS DROVE THE mules. The men talked, learning much about one another and about the area. Toots began to explain, "The story goes that a miner, fella name o' Baker, got into an argument with a Ute warrior or sub chief or somethin, name o' Colorow. Anyway, Baker loaded up his wagon and started high tailin' it outta there with Colorow hot on his heels, an' he tried crossin' the river, wrecked his wagon, lost a wheel, and there it stayed in the mud. An' cuz o' that, folks got to callin' the confluence of the Rio Grande and Goose Crick Wagon Wheel Gap, an' the name sorta stuck. Nowadays, there'a a few farmers and prospectors occasionally pass through, but ain't much. There's a few cabins an' the usual miner's tents an' such, but it has become sort of a crossroads."

Cord nodded and asked, "Didn't the Utes call this *Little Medicine* cuz o' the hot springs?"

"Yeah," answered Toots, frowning and looking at Cord with a stern expression, "How come you know that?"

Cord grinned, "Oh, I spent some time with Ouray and his people, learned a few things here and there. I think there's a bigger springs south of here, they call *Pagwöösa*. Both are considered holy places and have been a part of Ute history for some time."

"I heered that, yeah, an' don' the Navajo think the same way?"

"I believe so, but I'm not too familiar with the Navajo," answered Cord.

The canyon opened wide and the steep talus slopes on the north that fell from the basaltic cliffs high above, gave way to the flatter terrain with tall cottonwoods and willows thick along the banks of the Rio Grande. Across the river, more land showing farm fields, scattered cabins, and other structures told of early settlers, and before them the wide flats showed a few cabins close together that gave the appearance of the beginning of a town. Toots pulled the mules to a stop, pointed toward the few cabins, and said, "That'd be 'bout where I think I'll stop for now. Might open the store outta muh wagons, see if'n it'll make a place to stop permanent like."

As he spoke he saw a lone rider coming from the settlement, making his way along with a mule in tow. Toots shaded his eyes, frowning and mumbling, "I think I know this fella..." and watched as he drew near. He grinned, waved at the man and said, "Wal, howdy Spider! What'chu doin'? You ain't leavin'are you?"

The downtrodden rider scowled at Toots, frowned as he pushed his hat back and leaned on his pommel, "Ain't got no choice! They done took ever'thin' I had, and that was after I found some color. Thot I'd be makin' it big time, but the rapscallions of Wallace's bunch done took o'er ever'thing and takin' all the gold an' more. Ain't nobody safe. They done kilt ol' Woody an' Whiskers! After that, it done took the fight outta the rest of us. Them what stayed is kinda hidin' out." He growled and shook his head, pushing his hat back and scratching his touseled topknot. He glared at Cord, "Who's that you got with you?"

Toots grinned, "Aw, he's just a travelin' man I met a while back. He's a good'un, sure nuff!" and chuckled as he looked from Cord back to Spider.

"Whatchu got in them wagons?" asked Spider, nodding toward the two freight wagons.

"Gonna set up shop, maybe here, maybe some'ers else, don't rightly know yet."

Spider shook his head, pulled his hat down and said, "Good luck!" and dug heels to his horse and pushed down the trail. Cord and Toots watched him go, and Cord looked at Toots, "You sure about this? What he said doesn't sound too good."

"Ah, Spider was allus afraid of just about ever'thin'. That's why they call him Spider..." Toots chuckled as he began to explain, "He was sittin' round the fire drinkin' coffee and a itty bitty spider started up his pants leg an' he jumped up, knocked o'er the coffee pot, spilt his own coffee and ran off into the woods screamin' like a lit'l girl!" Toots grinned, slapped his leg as he laughed and remembered the event.

"So, I'll do as I said, but I'll keep muh gun right handy."

"Well, I might be around, too, maybe I'll see if I can be of any help," offered Cord. "But for now, I'm gonna look around. Kinda get the lay of the land and see what I might learn about the settlers as well as the outlaws. I'll find you later," he offered as he nudged Kwitcher to follow Blue who Cord had already motioned to the trail.

The gap itself was marked by the high-rising cliff faces that stood like sentinels on each side of the river. The long talus slopes were sparsely covered with serviceberry, rabbitbrush, sage, mountain mahogany, with patches of needlegrass, ricegrass, and wheatgrass. But the cliffs themselves were imposing and captured the attention of the bystander, both for the rock formations of granite, quartz, limestone, and more, and the teetering formations of stone that threatened to fall at the slightest provocation. But these were also the stones that held deposits of gold and silver and other metals, all drawing the attention of the prospectors of the day.

But Cord had been thinking about the hot

springs, remembering his time with the Ute people when they stopped at the hot springs in the San Luis Valley before their buffalo hunt. He had enjoyed hot springs before, the territory had many such, and after more than a week in the saddle, the thought of a hot water soak stirred his want-to's in his mind. Most hot springs have a distinctive sulphur smell, and he detected that same thing from the water of the feeder creek that flowed from a long valley that came from the hills to the south. Cord crossed back over the Rio Grande, where the freighter road had a shallow crossing and started up a dim trail beside what was called Goose Creek. To his left, the steep hills showed basaltic rim rock high above the valley floor, but off his right shoulder, the sun was cradled in a notch of black timbered hills that had a long skirt that fell from the high country and was riddled with runoff draws that showed aspen and juniper between the bald slopes. There were a few random cabins, a couple were empty, and one looked long abandoned, while nearer the creek and on the east bank, Cord passed three camps of prospectors with two having cabins.

Further upstream, he passed a farm that seemed to be doing well, crops in, fields showing green, and smoke coming from a cabin that lay in the shadow of a bigger barn. A few draws held trickles of creeks, but most were dry, until he was a little over a mile from the Rio Grande, and a teaser creek fell from the west and fed Goose Creek. A little further, another came from the east and did the same.

The smell of sulphur and the sighting of a thin column of steam betrayed the presence of a hot springs, and Cord nudged Kwitcher toward the sight. The pool sat lonesome on the flank of a ridged hill. A tall, long-dead snag of a tree reminded Cord of a story read to him by his father from Grimm's Fairy Tales. The tree looked like a lanky skeleton waving crooked arms to the sky. Cord chuckled at the thought, nudged Kwitcher past the pool to a draw of the hill where aspen betrayed the presence of a fresh-water spring. He made a quick camp, started a small fire, put on the coffee pot, stood, stretched, and looked about at the now shadowy valley in the dim light of dusk. He grinned and walked to the pool, tested the water, smiled, and after retrieving his rifle and some fresh clothes, he returned, stripped and slowly stepped into the pool, glancing back to where he had laid the rifle so it would be within reach in case of an unexpected visitor.

He found a spot where the bank fell into the water and offered a comfortable place to sit and lean back while he soaked in the soothing waters. He retrieved his rifle, brought it close and settled in to let his muscles marinate. He was lulled to a slight stupor but was brought back to consciousness by the rattle of hoofbeats. He came wide awake, looking through the vague steam, to see four men riding toward the settlement. They did not appear to be prospectors, dressed more like ranchers or hired hands with boots, chaps, and hats. He could not tell if they wore sidearms, but more than likely they would all be well-armed, especially after what Spider had reported.

Cord moved closer to his rifle, but the riders showed no recognition of the presence of another. Cord heard bits of conversation, but not enough to make any sense of what was said, although he repeatedly heard the name Wallace. The riders continued down the valley toward Wagon Wheel Gap, and Cord climbed from the pool, his nakedness bright in the beginning darkness of the night. He slipped on his trousers and was arrested by a voice that came from the shadows of the night. "You make a good target with your white skin."

It was not a threatening, but more of a humorous comment, as the speaker chuckled while Cord hustled into his clothes. He answered, "Depends on who's doing the shooting. Now if you're using that rifle I gave you, I'd probably be dead, but..." he shrugged as he looked into the darkness.

A buckskin-clad figure rose from the night and stepped into the light of the half-moon that hung high above. Cord grinned, held his arms wide as Lone Eagle of the Uncompahgre Ute people walked into his arms. She was the Puwagat, or Shaman, of the people, and had chosen Cord as her mate during the Bear Dance in the past. But Cord had to leave the village of the people and resume his duties as a deputy marshal, and Lone Eagle could not leave her responsibility as shaman for the people to be with him. But this was the land of the Uncompahgre Ute, sometimes called the Weeminuche Ute, and they were led by Ouray, who had been recognized by the White soldiers to be the leader of all the Ute.

She smiled up at Cord and said, "My people are coming here for the healing waters and to hunt. We will spend the rest of the summer here before returning to the lowlands. Will you be here long?"

Cord grinned, "Dunno. Just got here today and haven't had a chance to look around, or find out who's making trouble and such. But I'm in no hurry." He smiled as he pulled her near and they embraced. She leaned back, smiled at him and asked, "Will you camp with us?"

"Can't. I need to be busy and movin' about. No one knows I'm a marshal, and I wanna keep it that way for a while, at least until I find out who or what is behind the trouble."

"Our camp is near, you can come for a meal?"

"Sure, I can do that," answered Cord, as they stepped apart and he started gathering his gear to saddle up and join Lone Eagle and her people.

6

VISITORS

"Ouray will want to see you when they come," suggested Lone Eagle, as she stepped back from Cord's horse, looking up at him as he swung aboard.

"And I'll want to talk to him," replied Cord, settling into his seat, "when do you expect him and the rest of the band?"

"By the next moon," explained Lone Eagle, folding her arms across her bosom.

"That'll only be less'n two weeks, that soon?"

"Yes, they had already started when the Wolf-pack left to scout. We had summered here before and he expected us to scout it out, both for White men and for game."

"If I don't see them when they come through, I'll come back. But if I'm not here, you can find me among the settlement. There's been trouble and I have to get to the bottom of it soon. I might have to travel a mite, but I won't be gone long," explained

Cord, leaning forward on the pommel, "check with the trader called Toots. He's setting up his store so he'll be around, and I'll leave word with him."

He reached down and laid his hand on Lone Eagle's shoulder, "I haven't found out who's leading this bunch of outlaws, so I can't tell you who to trust, but Toot's is alright."

Lone Eagle nodded, letting a bit of a smile split her face as she touched Cord's hand before stepping away. She stood watching as he rode from their camp, thoughts of what might have been running through her mind as she allowed herself to linger by the trail.

THE FARMER'S field was empty, but smoke spiraled from the chimney of the cabin, and Cord rode on past. The sun was slowly climbing above the eastern mountains, but the long line of mountains off his right shoulder would keep this valley in shadows for a while longer. He passed two empty cabins, thought about making one his base and dropping his gear, but that could wait a day or two. As he neared the camp where the lone prospector had his canvas tent sat back near the trees, he noticed the tent was caved in and he saw no activity about. He casually reached down and slipped the thong off the hammer of his pistol, lifted the Remington to free it from the leather and nudged Kwitcher toward the camp.

He noticed there was no fire in the fire ring, no coffee pot nearby, and several things scattered about. With a quick survey that showed no one present, he stepped down and ground hitched Kwitcher, looped the lead of the mule around the saddle horn, and cautiously approached the tent. The front of the tent stood, the back was fallen in, and he pushed aside the entry flap and saw the booted feet of a man showing from under the remains of a blanketed cot. Cord pushed in, lifted the canvas and blanket, and the man stirred, mumbling and trying to move. Blood showed on his head, chest and hands. With a nearby stick, he propped up the canvas and knelt beside the man, lifting his shoulders and head.

"What happened here?"

The man struggled to open his eyes, and through slits, scowled at Cord, wincing at the pain. "Who... who're you?"

"I'm a federal marshal. My name is Cordell Beckett. What happened?"

"Wallace's men. Hit me last night, tore things up, shot me, beat on me, stole muh poke, but couldn't find muh hideout!" He tried to grin, winced and moaned. "How...how...bad?"

"From what I can tell, it ain't good, but I'll see what I can do. I'm gonna lay you down and get some things from my pack. What's your name?"

"Wilcott, Harold Wilcott. Been here since '68! Ain't leavin' yet!"

"Good. You hang in there, friend. I'll do what I

can." Cord gently laid the man down, using part of a rolled-up blanket for a pillow, then stood and walked from the tent. Wilcott had a bloody crease across the right side of his head above his ear where the bullet plowed through his thick hide. Another crease at the top of his right shoulder, and a through-and-through wound that cracked a rib on his lower right chest. After Cord had him cleaned up and bandaged, he was sitting up and trying his best to grin.

He looked at Cord, "You say you're a federal marshal?"

"That's right, but I don't want you tellin' anybody about that. I've got to do a little lookin' 'round first. And I think it would be best to move you away from here. I'm thinkin' that if those men find out you're still alive, they might wanna finish the job."

"You're prob'ly right, but what..." he started, but Cord interrupted.

"I think we can leave most everything here, undisturbed. Make you a lean-to back in the trees until you get a little better and can take care of your-self. You have any friends nearby I can send this way to look in on you?"

"Uh, yeah. Downstream there's another camp, a cabin with two fellas, brothers I think, name of Dunlap. Elmer and Elbert. They come into this country not too long after me, and we been sorta friends, you know how it is, when we're all lookin' for the same thing you don' wanna talk about par-tik-lars."

"Will they keep things quiet?"

"Shore. Whatever happens will affect them as much as me!"

When Cord rode up to the camp of the Dunlap's, they were busy at the creek, one shoveling ore into the long sluice box, the other watching the water wash the soil over the riffles. The second man held a rifle cradled in his arms, and he watched Cord approach. As Cord neared, the man raised the rifle to his shoulder, and hollered, "Best move on, stranger! Ain't nuthin' here for you! Go on! Move!" he ordered with a wave of the rifle.

Cord reined up, lifted both hands high, and answered, "I'm friendly, don't want nothin' but to tell you about your friend, Harold Wilcott!"

"What about him?"

"He got hit by some of who he called Wallace's men, and he's hurt pretty bad. I doctored him up, moved his camp, and said I'd ask you to check in on him now'n then. You're the Dunlap brothers, right?"

"Who's askin'?"

"My name's Cordell Beckett."

"What's your interest in this?"

"None. I just happened to find him. Saw his camp all torn up, din't like the look of it, rode close and found him, shot up and such. Doctored him, bandaged him, and moved him further back in the trees. Thought it'd be best if the one's that done it would still think he's dead so they'd leave him alone. That's why he needs somebody to check on him."

"Yeah, well, those same men came by here, but we run 'em off. Me'n muh brother know how to use these," motioning with his rifle—"an' we don' take no chances." The man with the rifle visibly relaxed, lowered the rifle, and said, "Beckett? Cordell Beckett? Seems I heard that name before. You been 'round chere?"

"Nope. First time hereabouts. Just passin' through."

The man frowned, started to lift the rifle again, "This ain't no place for passin' through. Ain't on the way to nowhere."

"You gonna check on your friend or not?" asked Cord, his impatience showing.

The man with the rifle glanced to his brother at the sluice, back to Cord and nodded, "Yeah, we'll check on him." But he quickly added, "But we ain't leavin' our claim empty nohow!"

"Wouldn't expect so. Thanks for checkin' on Wilcott. I might come back in a couple days to see how he's doin'. In the meantime, just so you'll know, the Uncompahgre Ute are movin' in upstream a ways. Gonna make their summer camp there, so don't get upset when you see them coming through here. They've been using this valley for a long time before you fellas came along." He nodded and nudged Kwitcher to move on down the trail.

Within a moment, the Dunlap brother called

after him, "Might check on them fellas downstream from us. We saw some smoke last night after those Wallace men passed through here. Mighta been their cabin. I think one of 'ems called Bishop or somethin'."

Cord waved, answered with, "Will do!" and nudged Kwitcher to a quick step trot.

A narrow point at the end of a long talus slope pushed the creek to the far side of the narrow valley, forcing the trail and Cord to ride around the point that showed a handful of piñon and sage clinging valiantly to the steep ridge. As he came in view of the next claim, thin tendrils of smoke rose from the charred remains of what had been a cabin. It was not a big cabin, Cord remembered it on his ride upstream, but it provided shelter and cover for the claimholders. The two men who had been working the claim would do so no longer. Their bodies lay near the cabin, clothes charred, flesh burned, and the stench of burning flesh filled the air. Cord slipped his neckerchief over his nose and mouth, pushed Kwitcher a little closer and stepped down.

As he neared, nothing moved, a mule stood hipshot in a small corral at the edge of the trees. The sluice box had been wrecked, shovels broken, pans scattered, and more damage to the lean-to and corral. Cord shook his head as he neared, checked the bodies for any sign of life, turned away and went to his mule for the shovel.

7

CONFRONTATION

THE GRAVES WERE MARKED WITH A CHARRED SLAB OF WOOD and charcoal writing, *Bishop and friend.* Cord rode from the grim site and pointed Kwitcher toward the settlement called Wagon Wheel Gap. The few buildings showed one to be a tavern and another as a hotel, if such could be called. It was no more than an extended cabin with a couple of added on rooms at the back. He spotted the two wagons of Toots and what appeared to be the makings of construction already beginning. Cord smiled at the thought of the man, always busy with something, having already made up his mind and beginning to set up shop.

The tavern was a log cabin, boardwalk in front, two windows and a set of swinging doors under the single sign saying, *Gap Tavern.* Cord nudged Kwitcher to the hitchrail, and after slapping the reins of the grulla around the rail, secured the mule's lead to the saddle horn and pushed his way into the tavern. He paused, letting his eyes adjust to the dim interior, then moved to the end of the plank bar, the plank suspended between two barrels with a barkeep behind the planks. The man sat a shot glass before Cord without saying a word, but Cord put his hand over the glass to keep him from filling it, looked at the man and asked, "Got'ny coffee instead?"The barkeep frowned, pulled the stub of a well-chewed cigar from his mouth, and said, "This is a bar, not a café!"

"Got'ny coffee in this bar?"

The man chomped on his cigar, nodded, and turned away to get an enamel cup and the coffee pot off the stove in the corner. He poured the cup full, sat the steaming black brew in front of Cord, and stepped back. "That'll be a nickel."

Cord nodded, dug out a shield nickel, and put it on the bar, holding it under his finger. "Might want another cup later."

The man nodded, pulled at the nickel, and pocketed it with a grunt.

Cord glanced around the small room that held three tables, each with three chairs, the bar that stretched across most of the end of the room that was only about twelve feet wide, and noted the four men gathered at one table, having pulled one of the chairs from another table. He recognized them as probably the four riders that passed his hot springs bath the night before and were also the same men that hit the prospectors. He turned back to the barkeep, "Been here long?"

"Couple years, longer'n most. Why?"

"Just wonderin'. Anybody make any strikes?"

"Nothin' worth talkin' 'bout. Some made a little, not many though."

Cord nodded toward the others, "Them fellas prospectors?"

The barkeep shook his head, lowered his voice, and said, "The only thing they prospect for is trouble."

Cord nodded and sipped at the coffee.

The four were huddled over their drinks, glancing occasionally toward Cord and mumbling among themselves. Suddenly, laughter erupted from the four, and the bigger man rocked back on the hind legs of his chair, slapped the table, making the empty shot glasses jump. He looked at Cord and back to his companions, looking for their laughter and agreement. He chortled, hollered for the barkeep, "Hey you! We need some more whiskey! Now!" and growled as he glanced from Cord to the barkeep.

One of the other men slapped his hand on the table and added, "Yeah! We got some more prospect-in'to be doin' an' its right hard work! Ain't that so, Brady?"

Brady leaned back in his chair, lifting the front legs off the floor again, rested his hand on the table and chuckled as he looked around at the others, nodding. He dropped down, leaned on the table and muttered something to the others, getting three nodding heads with conspiratorial mumbles from the men. Brady kicked back a nearby chair as he rose to his feet and threw his shoulders back, stretching to his full height which was about the same as Cord's six feet. He stomped over to the bar and stood beside Cord, glaring at the newcomer and growled, "Who're you an' whatchu doin' here?!"

Cord had seen their kind before, courage in a group, taking their strength from the others and encouraged by their goading and laughing. But if alone, they usually became quiet, reclusive, yet angry and evil still. Cord pegged the bigger man, Brady, as the leader. He was a big man, broad-shouldered, dark eyes that peered out from under heavy dark eyebrows, giving him an evil look, his leather vest was weathered and worn, but his holstered pistol showed clean, marking him as a careful man that took pride in his gun handling. Cord looked hard at the man, then turned away and reached for his coffee.

Brady leaned forward and stepped closer to Cord. "I asked you a question!"

Cord turned back to look at the man, looking him up and down as if sizing him for a box, and nodded, "Hmmm..." and turned back to his coffee.

The big man frowned, not understanding what this stranger was doing and not accustomed to anyone not paying full attention to him. He growled again, coughed, and said, "What'chu lookin' at, stranger? You just passin' through, or you gonna try to find some gold? Huh?"

When Cord did not turn nor respond, the big man growled and stomped his foot, slapped the bar, staggered a step, and moved closer and glared at Cord, realizing that this stranger was just as tall and probably just as wide as he was, and he did not show any fear. Brady dropped his chin, lifted the corner of his lip as he tried to snarl and growled, "I axed you a question!"

Cord had moved away from the bar, but faced the big blowhard and in an easy manner he answered, "If it's any of your business, I'm just passing through."

Brady glowered, growled, "Anything that happens 'roun' chere is my business! We be the boss o' this whole country!"

Cord chuckled, "And just how do you do that?" grinning as he looked at the man.

"Howsomee'er we want! An' what we do is nunya bizness, got that?" he growled, glaring at Cord, expecting the stranger to be easily intimidated.

Cord grinned, chuckled, and turned to face the man, "Oh, so if it's none of my business what you do, so how's it *your* business who I am and what I do?" He spoke in a light tone, not threatening. He added, "Don't make no difference to me, just curious is all." But he did not move nor look away.

Cord leaned his left elbow back on the bar, still

holding his coffee in his left hand and slowly stuck his thumb behind his belt buckle, flexing his fingers in the doing. His Remington Army pistol sat butt forward on his left hip, just inches from his hand. Cord let a grin split his face as he chuckled, and watched the big man's flustered reaction, knowing something was about to happen. Brady growled and cocked his fist back, ready to bring a roundhouse into his argument.

Cord saw it coming before Brady hardly moved, and without seeming to make a threatening move, Cord suddenly brought his elbow up and around to smash Brady's jaw, crashing the big man against the bar, making him stumble, grab his jaw, and slide to the floor. He whimpered. He lifted his bloody hand and stared with wide eyes, gasping for breath. He looked up at Cord who had stepped back, lifted his coffee for another sip, and looked down at the man on the floor.

The three at the table were startled to see Brady on the floor. They froze and fell silent as they looked astounded at their bully companion. Brady whimpered, "You bwoke it, you bwoke muh jaw!" He struggled to be heard and understood, but his eyes welled up with tears, and his face showed anger, and he struggled to get to his feet.

Cord said, "You might wanna take care of that. If it heals like that, you might not ever talk right again." He frowned with a serious expression as if he was genuinely concerned for the man, slowly shaking his head as he lifted his coffee cup for another sip.

Cord nodded, sat the cup down, and started for the door. The three at the table were frozen in place by the shock of seeing their leader downed so quickly. But a long skinny one started to rise, showing mostly legs and elbows beneath a pointed chin with patchy whiskers and under a beak nose. He was grabbing at his pistol, but the sight of the big Remington stopped him as he stared into the black hole at the muzzle of Cord's pistol that promised a gruesome death if he moved any further.

He glanced to his partners, both instantly slapping empty hands on the tabletop, and the skinny one said to the pot-bellied dirty one beside him, "Spence, check on Brady."

The second man slowly lifted his empty hands high as he rose, nodded toward the downed Brady, and started toward him. Brady was grabbing at the edge of the bar plank, bloody hand slipping, and Spence offered to help, but Brady waved him aside.

Cord glanced over his shoulder at Brady, saw him digging for his pistol, and Cord turned, his pistol in his hand and warned, "Don't do it!" as he cocked the Remington, the clicking of the hammer ratcheting, sounding loud in the room full of startled would-be toughs. Brady lifted his hand free of his pistol, leaned on the bar, and mumbled something about needing a drink to the barkeep, and turned his back to Cord.

When Cord stepped to the boardwalk in front of

the saloon, he looked up and down what folks were
calling the street, and to his right, he saw where
Toots was already at work erecting what would be
his store. Cord chuckled and took the reins of
Kwitcher and the lead of the mule, and with a wave
of Blue, started that direction.

8

SURVEY

THE STEEP TALUS SLOPE FELL FROM THE TOWERING basaltic and granite cliffs that stood imposing high above the valley floor, always looming over and shadowing the river bottom. Yet it stood like a big brother over the beginnings of the settlement that had assumed the name of Wagon Wheel Gap. Cord glanced about, taking in the sights of the few buildings that were taking shape among those that stood empty-eyed and watching, broken windows with shutters askew, telling of previous occupants that tried to make the makeshift cabin a temporary home, now housing nothing but varmints and rodents. Cord chuckled as he passed a broken-down log cabin, moved quickly past and approached the workers busy at making a false front for the newest tenant of the town, Toots Monroe and his general store that would offer supplies and more to the new arrivals.

"Wal, howdy Cord!" came a shout in a familiar voice as Toots stepped around the end of the front of the rising structure. He showed a broad grin, chuckled as he walked close, "So, I thought you'd be gone a few days, an' here it's only been a day and a lil' more! Find anybody you know?"

Cord stopped, slapped Kwitcher's rein around the hitchrail and leaned on the end of the post, "I did! Found some old friends, some folks that'll be your neighbors soon."

"Hey—suits me! The more people, the more business! Who they be?"

"The advance scouts of the Uncompahgre Ute people. They're called the Wolf Warriors or the Wolfpack. Their leader is a fella name o' Broken Arrow, and the shaman of the people is with 'em. She's an old friend, name of Lone Eagle."

"She? I thought their medicine men were men, you know, *men*."

Cord grinned, "Her daddy was, taught her, passed on and the people wanted her to do the job. She saw it as a great honor and has served them well."

As they spoke, one of the hired workers came near to talk to Toots and asked about the work to be done. Toots directed him about erecting the big tent behind the false front, adding, "After we get it up, then I'll set about gettin' some more timber and boards cut, then we'll finish the building as we can."

The man nodded, turned away, glanced back at Cord with a frown but moved on about his work.

Toots asked, "So'd, you see any prospectors or others that might be customers?" and chuckled as he leaned against the hitchrail.

Cord said, "Yes and no. I did see some prospectors, but right after a gang of outlaws struck and killed a couple, robbed 'em and left 'em for the buzzards."

Toots stood up straight, "You saw that? This mornin'?!" asked Toots, scowling.

"Ummhmm."

"Who dunnit?"

"You know anybody name o'Wallace?"

"Heard some talk, don' know him."

"What'd you hear?"

Toots stepped closer, glanced around and lowered his voice, "Nuthin' good, that's for sure."

The worker turned back and stepped closer, "I heard you say Wallace. You talkin' 'bout him or his men?"

"Some of his men. What do you know about 'em?" asked Cord, looking about for any others that might be within earshot.

"I've seen 'em, know they're poison mean. They kilt my partner, woulda kilt me, but din't know I was 'round. I hid in the trees while they ransacked our camp, broke our rocker, smashed ever'thing else 'fore they stole our stash. Muh partner tol' 'em where it was 'fore they kilt him."

"Anything else you know 'bout 'em?" asked Cord.

"Not sure, but I think the one called Wallace used to be a fella name o' Reynolds. He was one o' the Reynolds brothers that had a gang back home that terrorized the territory 'fore they was caught an' kilt. But one of 'em got away, an' I think Wallace is him."

"Seems like I heard of 'em. Where's *back home*?"

"O'er to South Park, 'round Alma an' such. Done some prospectin' o'er there a few years back, after I come home from the war. The Reynolds brothers led a band of guerrillas durin' the war, wore grey, they did. But when they was caught, ol' Chivington an' his men was gonna string 'em up, but John an' another'n got away. Folks said they went down to Santa Fe, but don' know fer sure."

The talker had paused, looked about and back at Cord, "Why you so interested?"

"Oh, I come on a couple camps that had been hit, miners killed and ever'thing stole."

"Today?"

Cord nodded, "Ummhmm."

The man nervously looked around as if he was going to see the outlaws hiding out nearby, but Cord said, "I don't think they'll be around here for a while."

Both Toots and Skeeter, the name Toots used for his worker, frowned as they looked at Cord, their expressions asking the question.

"We had a little set-to in the tavern yonder, nothin' much," answered Cord without any further explanation. He looked to Skeeter, "Anybody know where this Wallace might be? Or any more of his men?"

Skeeter shook his head, "Dunno, an' don' know anybody that does. If they did know, they prob'ly wouldn't say, ain't healthy, if' n you know what I mean." He frowned, looked at Cord, "Why you so interested?"

"Oh, just curious, I guess."

Toots frowned at Cord, looked to Skeeter and motioned him back to work and waited till he was on the far side of the structure before he looked at Cord, "What is it? You're up to somethin', I can tell."

Cord grinned, "Oh, nuthin' quite yet. Got some lookin' around to do. If Wallace or Reynolds or whoever he is, is around, I'd like to know where and who he is 'fore I do anything. So..." he shrugged. "For now, I think I'll find me a place to make camp and do some more lookin' around."

Cord stepped aboard Kwitcher, bent to pick up the lead of the mule, leaned on the pommel and looked at Toots. "What's going on around here is more than it looks. This guy Wallace or Reynolds or whoever he is, is after something and it's more than a few pokes from some hard luck prospectors. If he is Reynolds, back in the time of the Reynolds gang, this one and his brothers, they pulled some pretty big heists and accumulated a considerable fortune. And that fortune was never found and none of those that were hanged gave any information as to the location of their hideout. Now, it could be that this one, if he is John Reynolds, could be preparing to recover the loot from the gang's hideout place. So, if that word gets out, there will be every outlaw treasure hunter around coming up here and making things a whole lot worse than what it is already. I'm thinkin' it'd be best to round up these outlaws before word gets out about the hideout of the hoard of the Reynolds gang."

Toots had listened carefully to what Cord was saying, but he frowned and looked at the man. When he stopped, Toots asked, "But, ain't that what you'd be doin'? Just tryin' to find out where all that loot is hidden? Cuz, surely you ain't thinkin' 'bout doin' somethin' with the outlaws, like joinin' up with 'em or nuthin', are you?"

Cord chuckled, "No, I was thinkin' about roundin' 'em up, takin' back to Canon City and the territorial prison."

Toots frowned again, "But that ain't yore job, is it?"

Cord grinned, dug into his vest pocket and brought out the marshal badge, palmed it as he showed Toots, grinning all the while. "Now, don't you go tellin' anybody 'bout this, y'hear?" he cautioned.

Toots' eyes had grown wide as he looked from the badge to Cord and he silently shook his head, then mumbled, "Well, I'll be hornswaggled an' hog tied! If that don' beat all!"

"Nobody's to know, nobody! Not even your woman!" cautioned Cord as he pocketed the badge and looked sternly at Toots.

Toots looked up at Cord, let a slow grin split his face and chuckled. He pursed his lips, acted like he pinched them together, and nodded his head and watched as a grinning Cord rode away, bound for the high timber and a solitary campsite.

9

EXPLORING

WHEN CORD STARTED TOWARD THE CANYON, THE SHEER walls of the rimrock standing high above the black timber and the steep talus slope, his attention was captured by the thin line near the crest that split the dark grey of the rimrock. He had left the mule and his packs behind at the livery, preferring to make this scout brief and light. A smile split his face as he knew that was exactly what he wanted, a little stream that dropped in a waterfall and offered a pool at the base of the rimrock that would provide all the water he and his animals would need for a comfortable camp. He reined the big grulla to the skirt of the dark timber, thinking the towering spruce reminded him of a long line of Franciscan priests standing shoulder to shoulder, hooded heads bowed and hands folded in prayer. A faint game trail, unused for some time, flanked the timber and pierced the shadows but pointed to the thin waterfall that was his goal.

As he crested a timbered shoulder the trail bent around the shoulder and turned into the notch before breaking into a small park, a sudden loud crack made Cord grab the stock of his Winchester from the scabbard as he bailed off the big stallion and dropped behind a nearby boulder, both horse and dog looking at him like he had lost his mind. Cord frowned, listened, and when another report echoed across the valley and bounced around the rimrock cliffs, he recognized the distinctive sound and relaxed, went to the saddlebags to retrieve his binoculars. With elbows on the seat of his saddle, he scanned the edge of the cliffs across the notch and saw the faint trails that marked the rugged rocky faces. There on the edge of a slight shoulder, two big horn rams were squared off in their battle that would determine the leader of the small herd of bighorn sheep. He watched as both rams lifted up on their hind legs, head and horns cocked toward their foe, and in slow-motion, they leaned into their charge, then almost instantly smashed their big horns together, making a loud report that sounded much like a rifle shot. Cord grinned, as he watched for a moment longer, then cased the field glasses, and swung back aboard the saddle and nudged Kwitcher toward the thin white line and faint mist of the nearby waterfall.

The pool below the waterfall, although small, held deep crystalline water that showed the rocky bottom of the pool that appeared to have been carved by the falling water over eons of time. A thin trail of water led away and meandered through the trees toward the edge of the shoulder, and the sound from below seemed to be an echo of the waterfall above telling Cord there was another smaller water-fall below. On either side of the pool, tall grasses offered graze for his horse and a soft bed for Cord. With a broad grin of satisfaction, Cord stepped down and began stripping the gear from Kwitcher. Blue disappeared into the trees, but Cord knew he would not go any further than what he considered to be earshot, the dog never wanting to be very far away from Cord.

It was a comfortable camp, and the fire circle that had been used before, probably by natives, lay under the outspread branches of a tall spruce, assuring Cord of the dissipation of any smoke that would be a giveaway of his location. At the edge of the camp, a break in the trees at the shoulder of the little park also offered a location for Cord to scan the valley below and have a clear view of the main trail that led into the gap and through the gap into the higher reaches of the Rockies.

As he began to prepare his supper, he realized he was about to the end of his rations of meat and more, but that would give him an excuse to return to Toots' newfound general store, as well as the need to go hunting. He thought about the big horn sheep, but thought it would be easier to find a deer or even an elk rather than trying to climb up the rocky face of the cliffs to get a sheep and to pack out the meat. He had the most important staple, coffee, and he dug out the coffee pot and scooped up some clear water and returned to the little fire he had laid out and started.

Never one to be a late sleeper, Cord rolled from his blankets, rifle in hand as he looked about to see Kwitcher standing hipshot, head hanging, at the edge of the trees and Blue lay beside him, his head lifted and watching every move of Cord. He chuckled, reached for his boots and slipped them on, doffed his hat, and grabbed his Bible and rifle and started for the bald nob atop the shoulder where he planned to spend his time in prayer, study, and watching the breaking of day. The grey light of early morning offered enough light for him to see his way and when he dropped to the flat moss-covered rock, he smiled at the shadowy canyon below, listening to the sounds of early morning birds and the chuckling of the water from the falls and the river below. It showed all the promise of a good day and he leaned back on his outstretched arm and lifted his eyes to the sky that was beginning to show blue as the slow rising sun began to show its face far behind the hills and buttes of the land.

As the golden lances of early morning began to bend over the buttes, Cord closed his Bible and said his amen as he watched the curtain of darkness and shadows fold away and reveal the beauty of the valley below. The white water of the river rapids sounded their soulful music as they chased one another from the canyon, and the cry of a circling bald eagle high above added its staccato to the awakening day. Cord rose, returned to his fire and began preparing his fare of biscuits, bacon, and coffee.

With his appetite sated, Cord saddled Kwitcher, and after checking his weapons, swung aboard and gave Blue the wave to start on their way. He had taken a few minutes for another scan of the valley below and saw three riders come from town to follow the riverside trail upstream below him. As he watched with his binoculars, he could not recognize the men, but their horses, although not unusual, made him think these were three of the bunch that had attacked the miners the day before. He watched until they were out of sight below the shoulder of the mountain and decided to do some additional exploring today.

With Blue in the lead, they took a game trail that had a few fresh tracks of elk and maybe some bighorns, but the numbers were few. Keeping just inside the edge of the timber, the trail took them down the slope to a good watering spot at the river, one with lots of cottonwoods, alder, and kinnikinnick that would offer cover for any of the wildlife wanting water. When the trail crossed the wagon road, it dropped to the water, but Cord chose to follow the road after seeing the tracks of the three horses he saw earlier. Across the river, spruce and pine stood tall as if guarding the west bank of the Rio

Grande as it shouldered near the steep, rocky-faced butte that stood opposite the granite and basaltic cliffs on the east.

When the road broke from the gap, Cord saw the tracks of the riders where they left the road and chose a lesser trail that turned into a partially timbered gulch that lay in the shadows of another rim-rocked butte to the north. There had been others that had taken this trail, probably gold hunters, or it could be the trail to the camp of the Wallace gang, and these three were returning to their camp. Cord loosened the rifle in the scabbard, slipped his pistol from the holster and once again checked the loads as Kwitcher stepped out on the trail. The trail kept to the shoulder of the butte above the bottom of the gulch that showed a few prospect holes and miners camps. At each camp, the miners, usually in pairs, would have one holding a rifle while the other either panned or filled the rocker box with shovels full of soil and rock to be washed. But a quick look at the tracks on the trail showed the riders did not stop or leave the trail. Cord frowned and decided to stop at the next camp to talk to the prospectors.

The trail dropped to the bottom of the gulch before crossing over to take to the timber. Cord paused, stood in his stirrups and spotted a camp a bit higher up the draw and nudged Kwitcher that direction. When he spotted the tent, saw a couple men working a sluice, Cord stopped and hailed the camp. "Hello, the camp! I'm friendly! Can I come in and talk!"

"Keep your hands high and come on!" hailed the answer. And as was true of the other camps, one man stood with rifle in hand, carefully watching the strange rider approach. "That's close 'nuff! What'chu want?"

Cord settled back in the seat of the saddle, asked, "Can I put my hands down?"

"Go 'head, but be careful 'bout it. This shotgun ain't p'ticular 'bout when it goes off!"

As Cord crossed his hands on the pommel, he leaned forward, "You fellas been havin' any trouble with claim jumpers an' the like?"

"One. He's buried o'er there!" growled the shotgunner.

"That all? The reason I'm askin', I had a run-in with a group of 'em after I saw 'em hit a camp up toward the hot springs. They didn't like it much and I thought I saw the same ones on this trail earlier," he shared, as he nodded to the trail that led to the timber behind him.

"We've seen some riders, but there was two of 'em when they came here, an' when only one of 'em left, I reckon he spread the word that this camp was poison, so they ain't come back."

"How long ago?"

"Last week, why you so curious?"

"There's a man that has a reward on him, thought he might be in this area, and he's known to do his prospectin' with a gun. Name of Wallace. You hear 'bout him?"

The shotgunner frowned and asked, "You a head hunter?"

"No, but I've got a personal score to settle with him."

"Wal," began the shotgunner, visibly relaxing as he lowered the muzzle of the shotgun, "I've heard tell there's a bunch of 'em hangin' 'round with a fella by that name. Ain't seen him muh ownself, but he could be the one you're after. We've seen riders goin' up thataway," nodding to the trees, "an' comin' down toward the Gap an' such, but we stay purty busy our ownselves."

Cord nodded, "Well, thanks for the information. You fellas keep your guard up, these boys killed two miners yesterday and wounded another. Don't trust 'em or let 'em near. They're poison mean!" The shotgunner nodded and casually lifted his weapon as he watched Cord rein Kwitcher around and leave their camp.

———

SET back against the black timber stood a sod roof log cabin that showed its age. Probably built by trappers in years gone by, it had been built to last and had been taken over by the followers of the man who called himself Wallace. The corral beside the cabin held six horses and the top rail held saddles, blankets, and other tack. Three riders neared, went to the corral and stripped their mounts of the gear, adding it to the top rail with the others, and after using their hats to dust off their pants and more, they started to the door of the cabin that opened before they neared. Standing in the morning light was a big man with scruffy blonde hair, a whiskery face that held a few scars, the stub of a cigar hanging from thick lips and hands tucked into his belt. "Where's Brady?" called the man as he looked over the three.

The long-necked skinny one called Goose answered, "Shot himself!"

Blondy scowled, "No...Brady shot himself? What'chu mean?"

"Just what I said, he shot himself," continued Goose, as they neared the door and the blonde man stepped back inside. It was a larger than usual cabin with bunks lining the walls, a pot-bellied stove near the back wall and four men sitting at a plank table by the larger of two windows against the side wall. As the men entered, Blondy looked at the others, "You hear that? Goose said Brady shot himself!"

The men at the table turned toward the newcomers and one at the end of the table growled, "He did what?"

"Shot himself," repeated Goose, as the newcomers found seats on the bunks and two unoc-cupied chairs.

"Explain," ordered the obvious leader of the bunch, scowling at Goose.

"We hit a couple miners as we was comin' into town. Stopped at the Gap and was havin' a drink and this long fella come in, went to the bar and started askin' questions 'bout things. Brady din't like it, went to the bar to tell this fella 'bout it, but that fella hit Brady upside the head, broke his jaw, and knocked him down fer no reason at'all! An' Brady, when he came around, he couldn't move his jaw, couldn't hardly talk, whined and moaned about the pain, and we he'ped him outta the bar. But he set down on the boardwalk, holdin' his jaw and mumbled what we think was, 'I cain't stan' it!' and pulled out his pistol and blew a hole in his own head! Just like that!" and snapped his fingers as he sat on the edge of the bunk opposite the table.

"Then what'd you do?"

"Wal, we gathered him up, took out behin' the bar and dug a hole an' put him in it. Figgered he'd like bein' that close to the bar!" he chuckled.

"This fella that broke his jaw, what'd he look like?" asked Wallace, frowning at the three.

Goose glanced to the others, back to Wallace and answered, "Oh, nuthin' special. Kinda tall, good lookin' sort, good sized. But nuthin' special 'bout him."

"What does he ride?"

"Dunno, he left 'fore we could get Brady outside. Din't see him after that."

Wallace glanced to the others at the table, back

to the three and asked, "These miners you hit, get anything?"

"Ummhmm," answered Goose, digging for the pouches he had in the saddlebags he slung over his shoulder. When he found them, he tossed them to Wallace.

Wallace looked at the leather pouches, hefted them, looked back at the three. "That's it? Three pouches of dust?" he asked, showing his contempt for the three.

"Ummhmmm," answered Goose, looking at the other two and back to Wallace. "All they had. Ain't been there long, but we got it all," he added, grinning.

With a nod to the man across the table, a pistol roared and Goose blossomed red on his chest, fear on his face, as he crumpled to the floor. Wallace looked at the others, "You two will split up with these four, after you take out that trash!" nodding to the body on the dirt floor.

10

FRIENDS

CORD KEPT TO THE TREES WHERE SEVERAL FAINT GAME trails offered passage through the pines and spruce, yet close enough to the tree line to see movement on the trail below. The trail he followed rode high on the west-facing shoulder opposite the rocky face of the canyon wall beyond the creek bottom. There was no movement nor sound from below, the only break in the monotony of silence was the whispering breeze in the pines or the shuffle of Kwitcher's hooves in the pine needles. But Cord was uneasy, reined up and scanned the woods beyond and below, turned in his seat to look above into the darker timber that clung to the high side of the rolling hill, and nudged Kwitcher into the darker timber to take to the high ground. But a slight smell of smoke made him rein up, stand in his stirrups and look a little more carefully through the thick timber, but the trees stood close about and refused to yield to his prying eyes.

He gave Kwitcher his head and let the big grulla pick his own way through the trees as the heavy-boughed spruce gave way to the tall lodgepole pine that stood apart from one another and held their branches aloft, allowing easy passage and views as they climbed the face of the big hill. Kwitcher made a bit of a switchback and picked his way along the face of a high bluff, rounded the crest and topped out high above the valley floor. Cord stopped the eager grulla stallion before breaking from the trees, made a quick scan of the open hillside, then again gave Kwitcher his head.

When the big stallion crested the low shoulder behind the higher bluff, he turned back to the north-west and moved across a saddle and dropped into the edge of the trees and stopped, bending around to look at his rider as if to ask, "Well?" Cord chuckled to himself and swung to the ground, rifle in hand, binoculars hanging around his neck, and he ground tied his four-legged friend and moved to the slight rise and bellied down beside a twisted cedar, his belly on the moss-covered boulder. He had spotted the thin spiral of smoke that came from the lower edge of the trees, and with his binoculars, he saw the movement of several horses in a corral beside a sod covered cabin. The trees would not allow a good count of the horses, but Cord recognized the blaze-face sorrel as one of the horses ridden by the three men that came from town. He grinned as he continued to scan the area around the cabin, knowing this was probably where the rest of the Wallace gang would be found, but he was not ready to move against them.

Cord sensed rather than heard the presence of someone near. His rifle was close at hand, and he moved only his eyes as he slowly lowered the binoculars. If he moved, he might give himself away as movement always catches the eye of a careful observer. He was somewhat shielded by the overhanging branches of the twisted cedar, but he knew he was exposed to anyone from above him on the crest of the hilltop. He had not expected anyone to be higher or to approach from behind him, and that assumption just might get him killed. He slowly took a deep breath, starting to let the binoculars hang free around his neck as he reached for the rifle, but a voice stopped him with, "No, do not move!"

It was a soft-spoken command from a familiar voice that Cord instantly recognized as he responded, "Hello Broken Arrow, my friend and brother."

A low chuckle came from behind him as he heard the soft steps of moccasined feet approach. "How have you lived so long? I watched you come through the timber and take your place, and you did not even look to see me or the others?"

"Others?" asked Cord, as he rolled to his side and brought his knees up to come to his feet. He stood, looked at his friend, the leader of the Wolfpack Warriors of the Uncompahgre Ute people, and saw two others behind him. One, a familiar face of a younger man, the other a slightly familiar face of a woman he had seen before, but not as a warrior. She scowled at the White man and turned away, going to their horses that stood at the edge of the trees. He looked back at Broken Arrow and asked, "Who are your companions?"

Arrow stretched out his hand to the young man, "This is Hawk that Soars. He has become a proven warrior and was chosen to join the Wolfpack."

Cord nodded, clasped forearms with the young man and turned back to Arrow, "And that one?" nodding to the woman that was with the horses.

Broken Arrow grinned, "That is Coyote Howling. She was a White woman captured long ago and chose to remain with the people. She had a man, but he was killed on a hunt by a big grizzly, and now she has chosen to ride with the Wolfpack."

Cord nodded, glancing toward the woman and back to the grinning Broken Arrow. Cord frowned, "So, what's that all about?" referring to his grin and laughter.

"Did you see the necklace of claws she wore? When her man was attacked by the grizzly, she was there. She picked up his bow, emptied the quiver of arrows into the big bear, then finished him off with her skinning knife. She came back into camp with the hide of the bear around her shoulders and told no one what had happened. My warriors went to find her man, and the story was told by the tracks and carcass. She was alone, chose to follow the path of the warrior, and the Wolfpack asked her to join with us. She has proven herself many times and is one of the most respected of our warriors."

"So it's best to stay out of her way, huh?"

"Yes."

"She doesn't look all that..." Cord frowned, trying to think of a descriptive term for the woman. She was not a big woman, did not have any masculine features, but was not a frail-looking female either.

Broken Arrow looked at Cord, turned away from the others, and looked below, "What is it you look for?" nodding to his previous perch.

"There are some men, outlaws really, that are in the cabin below. I had a run-in with them in town, and I thought they were with a bigger group and they are together down there. They've killed a few prospectors, stolen their gold, basically trying to run everything in the valley, but I've been sent to put a stop to it all."

Broken Arrow frowned, "As a marshal for the White man?"

"Ummhmm." Cord palmed his badge, "When I was given this, it was to help me find the men I was after, those that killed my family. I did that, but I had promised to fill the duties of a deputy marshal and Marshal Sheffenberg came down from Denver and asked me to take over this part of the territory and try to bring peace and law to the area. He expects there to be more White men coming here, looking for gold."

"But this is our land. It was told us in the last treaty time that all the land west of the mountains was to be the land of the Ute—the Uncompahgre, Weeminuche, Muache, and Capote. Even the White River Ute are west of the mountains but north of our land. This is not the land of the White man, but of my people."

"I know that Broken Arrow, that's why I'm here. I want to rid this land of not just the outlaws, but all White men because they have broken the treaty, but first, I need to deal with the outlaws. They're a bunch led by a man that calls himself Wallace, at least for now."

"Ouray has said the White men are wanting a new treaty and want us to leave this land, but it has not been settled yet. You remember he has said he wants you to talk with him and to talk for us at the treaty time."

"I remember, and I will do that. But first, I have this to do."

Broken Arrow dropped his eyes, started to turn away, and Cord added, "Tell your sister I will come see her soon. But my camp is..." he started to tell the location but stopped when Broken Arrow grinned and held up his hand to stop Cord.

"We know where you camp. We have watched you, and our people know where you are and what you do. If you need help, let us know. Someone is always near."

Cord frowned, then let a slow grin cover his face as he nodded and watched his friend return to his horses and the three of them leave. It was not surprising to him that they knew where he was camped nor that they kept watch for him. They had become like family to him, and he was thankful for their friendship, especially in this land where there were few friends to be found, and more than enough that opposed any form of law or lawman.

He returned to his perch and stretched out in the shade to continue his watch. He had no sooner lifted the binoculars than he saw a horseman dragging something behind his horse and away from the cabin. The rider went toward the gulch in the bottom of the draw, reined up, and went to the dust-covered bundle behind him and removed the lariat. As Cord watched, he saw the parcel was a man's body, and the rider rolled it over and into the gulch, stood above it, looked about, and mounted up to return to the cabin.

Cord shook his head, knowing the outlaws had apparently had a falling out of sorts and at least one of them had been forcibly excluded from the gang. He still did not know how many there were and thought he might work his way closer, but decided to just maintain his vigil from this distance. He mumbled to himself, "My momma din't raise no fools!"

AFTER SEVERAL HOURS on the promontory and with
little activity around the cabin, Cord chose to make
his way closer to learn more about his adversary. His
time with the Ute people as well as his experience as
a man hunter, taught Cord the ways of the woods
and he now moved with silence. Always carrying a
pair of moccasins in his saddlebags, he left Kwitcher
tethered and now moved through the shadows of the
pines. He chose to approach the cabin from the high
ground, staying in the black timber and only getting
near enough that with the help of his binoculars, he
could see the men, learn their numbers and a bit of
their ways. He chose a cluster of spruce with low-
hanging branches and nearby juniper brush. He
bellied down, crawled under the low branches and
took up his vigil.

Three men were at the corral, two tending to the
horses and one fiddling with the tack hanging on the
top rails. The men in the corral were two he had seen
in town. Cord was near enough to hear some of the
talk, for sound, especially talking, carries well in the
thin mountain air of the high country. As he watched
and listened, he heard the man at the rail call the
men Snake and Spence. Cord chuckled as he looked
at the two and guessed the one called Snake was the
pot-bellied one with snake eyes, heavy whiskers, and
wore all black. That would make the second man
Spence, who was always digging at himself, wore

tattered trousers that were held up by galluses. The man at the rail answered to the name of Blondy, and Cord thought him to be a more formidable type. Tall, broad-shouldered, whiskers marked with scars, a stub of a cigar in his teeth and a holstered pistol, another tucked in his belt and a knife at his back.

Movement at the corner of the cabin caught Cord's eye and a tall man came from within and hollered at the three at the corral. He was a big man, broad-shouldered, easily over six feet tall, and topped the scales near two hundred fifty pounds, none of it fat. His black hair had a streak of white that came from above the left eye and over his ear, giving the man an evil stare with a streak of mean-ness about him. He growled at those at the corral, "Wallace says for you to saddle our horses an' get ready to ride!"

"Which ones you want, Brown?" asked the shifty-eyed Snake, snarling at the bigger man.

"Wallace takes the black, mine's that tall bay, and Johnny's the blaze-face bay! Get a move on! Boss is inna hurry!"

The mumbles came from the two in the corral but the one at the rail, Blondy, answered as he glared at the two, "You two better get a move on—you saw what the boss does to those that buck him!"

11

SKIRMISH

CORD SLOWLY BACKED FROM UNDER THE SPRUCE, CAME TO his feet, and quietly padded away to return to the crest of the hill where Kwitcher was tethered. Blue came from the shadows and trotted at his side. Cord chuckled to himself, comfortable with knowing the dog was always near and would be an added protection. He swung aboard the big grulla, slipped the rifle into the scabbard, and dropped the binoculars into the saddle bags as he started back to his camp. Now he knew there were seven men, but there could be more.

He cataloged them in his mind by their names and the descriptions and possibly by their horses as well. And he knew they were riding away from the cabin, but he didn't think they would be leaving, maybe going on a raid somewhere, but Cord was not ready for a confrontation, so he would not follow. Although, the thought of their eagerness to make another assault on some unsuspecting prospectors or others rankled. It was not his nature nor habit to avoid a fight, but this was different. He would be acting in his official capacity as a deputy marshal, and he had to try to take them alive and haul them to court and probably back to Canon City to the territorial prison. All that would require more than just a steady hand with a pistol or rifle.

But instead of going back to his camp, he turned back to the north, thinking he wanted to get the lay of the land and know the territory, and the only way to do that was to take the time to give it a good looking over. He was atop a long butte that was sided by runoff creeks that fed the Rio Grande, and as he broke from the trees, he was above the camp of the outlaws and crossed a bit of a saddle that afforded him a look at the two canyons that carried the creeks. To his right, or northwest, he saw a smaller creek in the narrow canyon that showed towering rimrock on the south side and a steep talus slope on the north. To his left, a deeper and narrow gorge that lay between rimrock and cliff lined walls on either side, while the creek below carried water over a series of rapids and waterfalls, with the crashing of waters echoing through the gorge. Neither canyon offered a trail to the bottom, so Cord turned back south, but kept closer to the north canyon, hoping for a break in the rimrock that would afford a trail to the bottom.

It was crowding noon with the blazing summer sun unhindered by any clouds and the heat bouncing off the black basaltic rock of the rimrock, making Cord seek some shade in a cluster of aspen that clung to the steep-sided hill below. The white-barked trees held high their pale green leaves that seemed to applaud Cord's arrival and he doffed his hat, wiped his brow and let Kwitcher have his head knowing if there was water nearby, he would find it and true to his nature, the long-legged grulla pushed through the trees to a little spring-fed pool and dropped his nose into the clear cool water. Cord swung down and dropped to one knee beside Blue and scooped up some cold water, all the while watching the area about them. A pair of magpies cawed their protest to the intruders, and a golden eagle circled high overhead and added his screeching protest.

Cord loosened the cinch on the grulla, dug out some jerky from the saddlebags and sat back against the bigger aspen and let the horse graze. Blue trotted about, sniffing the ground and searching the grove but had no luck finding any available game. He returned to Cord's side and stretched out beside him, lifting his sorrowful eyes to the man as he begged for a bite of jerky, and he was not disappointed. Cord rubbed the dog's head and ears as he looked around, but his reverie was interrupted by the rattle of distant gunfire. He came to his feet, but he knew the rifle fire was well away from him and further below in the canyon and undoubtedly further downstream toward the Rio Grande. He looked at Kwitcher who stood head raised, ears forward as he too looked toward the gunfire. Cord chuckled, "Well boys, reckon our noon break is over, so..." and shrugged as he tightened the cinch and stepped aboard Kwitcher and motioned Blue to scout the trail off this butte.

The dog knew to keep to the edge of the trees, but the wide runoff draw opened to a bald face of the butte that stood between Cord and the rifle fire beyond. Blue paused, looked over his shoulder to see Cord motioning him to the tree line on the shoulder to the north, and Blue took off at a run. Cord dug heels to the grulla and within moments they were behind Blue as he stood, head down, one paw lifted as he looked over the saddle of the hill toward the bottom of the canyon beyond. Cord dropped to the ground beside him, field glasses in hand and took a long look below. It was about a quarter mile to the canyon bottom where he saw the scene of the commotion. One man was belly down, blood showing on his back, another stood between the narrow creek and a wall tent, hands raised, while two or three men were rummaging through the gear and tent. A sluice box had been overturned and smashed, other gear scattered. Four others sat their saddle, two with rifles trained on the standing prospector.

Cord made a quick look around and returned to Kwitcher. On one side, Cord carried his Winchester in a scabbard, and on the other, in a similar scabbard was his Spencer. He grabbed the Spencer, checked the load and dug out some more cartridges from the

saddle bags and motioned Blue to stay with Kwitcher
and started through the trees, quickly making his
way down the slope to a promontory that stood
above a cluster of rimrock overlooking the narrow
canyon and the site of the trouble.

Cord quietly worked his way through the trees,
dropped to a crouch, and went to the shoulder of the
promontory and bellied down. Now less than two
hundred yards from the others, he adjusted the telescopic sight, checked his load, and picked his target.
Preferring not to kill anyone outright, he just wanted
to make his presence known and that he could bring
death to call. He chose one of the riflemen that sat on
his horse, the rifle held carelessly before him, the
forestock resting on his saddle horn. Cord narrowed
his sight, took a breath, held it, slowly let it out as he
squeezed off the shot. The big Spencer roared,
bucked, and spat lead and fire to send the messenger
of death to shatter the stock of the man's rifle. The
boom of the big Spencer echoed across the canyon,
bouncing around the granite walls and magnifying
the fright and confusion. They could not pinpoint
the shooter with the rattling echoes bouncing
around.

The cacophony of sound spooked the three
frightened horses, the man on the blaze-faced bay
grabbed the horn, jerked on the reins, and tried to
take a deep seat as the horse climbed into the air,
bent in half, and tucked his head between his front
feet before hitting the ground again. The rider lost

his grip and seat and tumbled over the horse's head to plant his face in the mud on the creek bank.

The second man that also held a rifle, dropped the weapon, grabbed reins and the saddle horn as his horse took off to the races heading upstream and crashing through the thick timber. Just before the horse disappeared into the black timber, Cord saw the rider get swept clear of the saddle by a strong limb of a big spruce.

The third man had both hands free and pulled tight on the reins, lifting his horse's head before he could tuck it and buck. With his feet deep in the stirrups and pulling with all his strength, he quickly brought his horse under control, but the other three that had been riderless, quickly disappeared in three directions. One took to the trees and began climbing the steep hillside, another went downstream kicking and bucking all the way and the third followed the now riderless one into the trees upstream.

Cord was amazed at the rodeo before him, but chuckled as he jacked another round into the Spencer and cocked the hammer for another shot. The man with the shattered rifle was crawling out of the creek, and the one on the black horse bent low to stroke the horse's neck, apparently calming the animal, but as he straightened up, he had a rifle in hand and was searching the hillside for the shooter. The men that had been rummaging through the prospector's gear had grabbed their pistols but those would be useless at this distance, and Cord focused on the rider.

Knowing the rider had no idea where the shots came from, Cord waited for a better shot. As he watched, the men were talking and searching the hillsides, and Cord noticed the miner who had stood with hands raised, had disappeared. The rider barked orders to the others, and they soon scattered in the hunt for their own horses, leaving the rider alone. Cord chose a target, the creek bank just beyond the black horse, but decided to put the round under the horse. As he squeezed off the shot, the bark of the big gun echoed across the canyon, and the horse almost took flight – coming off the ground and twisting like a snake, his head and front legs going one way, his back legs the opposite. The broom tail waved like a flag from a pirate ship, the stirrups bouncing like a witch's broom on Halloween. The big black was intent on his own freedom and soon loosed the rider who had kicked free of the stirrups, clung to his rifle, and hit the ground in a roll. The man quickly came to his feet and fired a shot where Cord had been, but Cord had already chosen his next shooting position, and from beside the rimrock ledge, he fired a round that plowed mud and rock in the face of the shooter.

Cord rolled away and into the trees behind him, stood behind the big trunk of a ponderosa, found a target, sent a bullet to plow a groove across the outlaw's neck and rip the neckerchief away. Cord called out, "Wallace! Or Reynolds or whatever you're calling yourself—take those no-good bums with you and leave the country. Next time I'm gonna shoot to kill! And I'll start with Blondy there, then maybe Dixie, or Johnny, or Brown. If you're still around by sundown, every time I pull the trigger, one of you will die!"

As expected, a barrage of bullets tore through the trees seeking out their target, but Cord had already dropped behind the big ponderosa and disappeared into the rocky terrain covered with trees, shrubs, and boulders. He knew he was well behind cover and that his taunt would only make Wallace more angry and determined to kill him, but that would at least keep them away from the unsuspecting prospectors and give Cord an opportunity to lower the odds. He crested the saddle crossing, grabbed the reins of Kwitcher and swung aboard, Blue at his heels as he started back to the northeast, keeping to the edge of the timber and using the carpet of pine needles to mask his passing.

Cord was certain a man like Wallace, determined to exert his will on others and take what he wanted, would not allow that surprise attack to dissuade him from his ways. He would have to pursue his unknown attacker and kill him, or he stood to lose what little loyalty his men had learned. If he was not the baddest bull in the woods, they would find another or try to show themselves as a leader of the band.

Cord also wanted to learn more about the country around this corner of the territory that had become his assigned region when Marshal Sheffenberg had asked him to take over this, the third district of the territory of Colorado. He needed to know the terrain, the trails, the people, and more if he expected to do the job he had accepted and do it well.

The lay of the land showed a wide park off to his right that rose to the edge of a big horseshoe-shaped butte that bent around in front of him and was crowned by tall peaks of the San Juan range beyond. To his left, or the northwest, the steep-shouldered butte fell away with black timber covering the slopes before offering a flat shoulder of timber that stretched a little over a half mile toward the northwest before falling into the canyon of the headwaters of East Bellows Creek. Although Cord did not know the name of the creek, he would later learn that this was the east fork and that both the east and west fork originated in the foothills of the San Juan's, and both cut deep canyons as they carried the spring runoff from the heavy snows of winter.

A glance off his left shoulder told Cord it was time to find cover and a camp before dusk lowered its final curtain. A grove of aspen beckoned and whispered the possibility of water, and he pointed Kwitcher to the white-barked trees whose leaves were waving a welcome. Cord had always been careful at choosing a campsite, wanting comfort but preferring a site that afforded cover over comfort, and this one fit both bills. A grassy flat at the base of big ponderosa on the uphill side promised a soft bed of long pine needles and overhead cover of long branches, while the thicker aspen would sound a warning with the dry leaves warning of any intruder. A break in the aspen also afforded a view of any approach, and beyond the flats was a long, empty park that was fringed on the west by scrub oak and more that stood atop the rimrock that overlooked the canyon below.

Cord stepped down and began stripping the gear from his horse, relieved he had brought the mule and other gear and supplies. He shook his head and grinned as he resolved himself to a night of cold jerky, warm blankets, and comfortable sleep.

12

RECONNOITERING

AFTER REACHING THE HEADWATERS OF EAST BELLOWS
Creek, Cord rode in the shadows of the San Juans and
rode along the skirts of glaciers before taking to the
west rim of another creek that he would learn later
was West Bellows Creek. This was higher altitude
and the pines that colored the steep hillsides were
the skinny lodgepole pine and the rugged bristle-
cone. He watched the country and his backtrail
constantly. At the first sign of diggings along the
creek below, Cord dropped off the butte to take a trail
that sided the creek and brought him to the abandoned site of recent diggings. But there was no sign
of any foul play, just those of a disappointed
prospector that left a broken and rusted shovel, the
remains of a hand-built shaker box, and evidence of
a wall tent.

Cord chose to stay near the creek, keeping to the

timber whenever possible, wanting to sound the warning to any of the miners in the area. And he had not traveled far when a hail rang out and warned, "Don't come any closer or you'll get a belly full of buckshot!"

Cord reined up, lifted his hands, "I'm friendly! I'm alone and I've come to warn you 'bout some outlaws!"

"Get down an' come in with yore hands high!" answered the shotgunner.

Cord did as he was told, Kwitcher and Blue close behind. As he neared the camp, he explained, "My name is Cord. Just wanted to let you and any others know there's a gang of outlaws killin' an' looting prospectors. They follow a fella calls himself Wallace."

"What's it to you? Why you tellin' us 'bout it?" asked the shotgunner who still held the two-eyed mankiller trained on Cord.

"They jumped me, too! Even though I'm not a prospector, but I came on 'em attackin' another fella, kinda put the fear in 'em, and hightailed it outta there. There's seven or eight of 'em, and I'm thinkin' their way of doin' things is for a couple to ride up, get down and start things 'fore the others join in. They've killed a few already, and they won't hesitate to shoot." As Cord spoke, two other men came from the trees, one with a rifle in hand, the other carrying a shotgun.

"Yeah, we heard some o' that. Know any o' them that got kilt?" asked the shotgunner.

"No, but it was up toward the hot springs," answered Cord, then added—"Can I put my hands down?"

The man snickered, looked to his companions for assurance, turned back to Cord, "Yeah, go 'head 'n drop 'em, but don't try anything."

A relieved Cord dropped his hands, keeping them from his weapons and reached back for the reins of Kwitcher, "I'll be leavin' then. I'm goin' down the creek—will I find any others?"

"Yeah, there's several. Leastways they was there last time we were downstream. Ain't got much reason to go nowheres since there ain't no place to get supplies," grumbled the man.

Cord chuckled as he swung aboard, "There is now. A fella name of Toots is puttin' in a general store down at the Gap. Prob'ly has it up an' runnin' by now. Good man, has a good supply. I rode with him a spell. He had two big freight wagons full!" Cord gave a wave and nudged Kwitcher back to the trail.

Cord came upon three more claims that had men working at finding some color. One was just above the confluence of the west and east forks of the creek, one just below, and another one about halfway down the wide open gulley of the creek before it joined the Rio Grande. He had about the same reception at all three, at least one armed man on guard and one or two others working the claim with either sluices or rockers, none admitting to finding any color. Although that was a common response, Cord judged by the skittishness of the workers that all were protecting what they already found or were optimistic as to the findings already.

When creeks merged with the big river, Cord broke out into the wider valley of the Rio Grande and stopped for a good look around. Keeping near cover, he sat beside a cluster of tall fir, and with the accompaniment of the musical Rio Grande River, he reveled in the beauty of the land. On either side of the river, set well back, rose smaller foothills. Those on the east side showed exposed shoulders of stacked sandstone, steep hillsides with sage and mesquite clinging to the slopes, and piñon and juniper at the crests. Most of the exposed flanks showing white splotches of calcite. On the west side, the rolling hills were mostly timber covered with spruce, fir and pines, with broad splashes of the pale green leaves of the aspen groves that in the fall would show brilliant gold. The riverbank on the west also held tall lodgepole pine, straight spruce, and low-growing kinnikinnick and cranberry bushes. The waters of the Rio Grande appeared crystal clear with splashes of white where the water tumbled over the rocks and offered hiding places for the many cutthroat and brown trout.

The hills stood like protective big brothers all along the river, standing well back and allowing wide swatches of gramma fill flatlands for the elk, deer, and an occasional antelope to take their fill. It was a beautiful valley, but the visitors through this land were not looking for scenery, and were always willing to scar those same hillsides with prospect holes in their search for riches, leaving behind refuse, trash, and scars to tell of their passing. Cord took a deep breath, and nudged Kwitcher to the flanks of the hills on the west edge of the valley, preferring the cover of black timber to the convenience of fresh water and the roar of the river.

But in his reverie and the immersing of himself in the beauty of God's creation, Cord had failed to see two men downstream and in the cottonwoods that spotted him when he came from the valley of the feeder creeks. While he paused to take in the views, the two men had a pair of binoculars trained on him, and recognized him as the man from the bar that had broken their friend's jaw. Spence lowered the binoculars, handed them to Snake and said, "That's him, alright. We better find Wallace and tell him."

As Snake watched their quarry, he asked, "Why don't we just take him an' tell Wallace after?"

"Huh? You crazy? Even if we could, do you think Wallace'd be happy 'bout it? He'd wanna nail our hides to the wall!"

"Nahh...we can just foller him, spot his camp, wait a bit, sneak up on him, and take his scalp. When we get back to the cabin an' tell Wallace about it, he'd be tickled, and we could do whatever we wanted to after that. We'd be better'n Brown, or Barnes, or any of 'em! That'd also give us a better cut o' the takin's! An...an...he told us to find him, an' din't say we couldn't take him!"

Spence was against the whole idea until Snake mentioned getting a better cut. He had seen that happen before, whenever one of the others or even a group of the others came back with more takin's than the others, Wallace would always give them a better cut than the rest. Greed is always a common trait of the wicked, and Spence probably had more than most. He looked at Snake, thought about it just a moment, then said, "Then don't lose sight of him! We prob'ly oughta go up on that hillside yonder where we can get a better looksee!"

———

CORD HAD A COLD CAMP, no fire, no smoke, and still he was feeling like there was something out there. He had watched his backtrail and was confident no one had followed him from the confluence of the creeks or the confluence of the creeks with the Rio Grande, but he also knew he could have been spotted when he crossed the open flats after crossing the river and heading for the timber. On a hunch, he stuffed his blankets with a couple heavy branches of pines, moved away from the bedroll, and found a point of vigil in the thicker timber. He sat back against the crusty bark of a spruce, checked the loads in his pistol and crossed his arms as he lowered the brim of his hat low over his eyebrows, allowing himself to still see the camp below. Blue lay at his side in the darker shadows, the moonlight scarcely penetrating the thick timber.

It was a still, quiet night. The halfmoon riding a carpet of wispy clouds yet sharing most of its light that penetrated the thick timber in thin shafts of yellowish grey. About two hours after leaving his bedroll, Cord heard the rattle of a small stone tumbling down the hill, but that could be from anything caused by any number of night creatures. But the crunch of a broken branch and the whisper of footfalls on the thick carpet of pine needles told Cord this was not the typical nocturnal hunters. This was not from a wolf, raccoon, fox, or anything of the sort. This was from the lowest of night crawlers, a two-legged outlaw.

Cord slipped the big Remington pistol from the holster, slow in all his movements, although he was well masked by the darkness and the deeper shadows of the timber. He saw the movement of two men, trying to be stealthy in their approach, both with guns held before them that caught and reflected the minimal light of the moon, and watched as they neared his camp.

Suddenly, the quiet of the night was shattered by the roar of two pistols blasting and stabbing flame in the darkness as they repeatedly shot into the bedroll of their target. When they stopped, one shouted,

"We got him! We got him! An' lookee yonder, we get his horse too!"

Cord had risen, stepped closer, but they were unaware of his presence until he spoke softly, "You ain't gettin' anything you don't deserve!"

Both men turned and swung their pistols as they moved, but Cord's pistol blasted and sent two bullets to pierce the filth of each man before him. Although they brought their pistols to bear, both hammers fell on empty chambers and the sudden impact of bullets brought horrified stares to the faces of the men, followed by the melting of their faces as they looked down and grabbed at their chests to see blood course through their fingers. One of the two, Spence, looked up at Cord and said, "You kilt us!"

"Nope, you done that all by your lonesome."

"Who are you?" asked Snake, fear in his eyes as he dropped to his knees.

"Deputy Marshal Cordell Beckett!"

The men tried to look at one another but fell to the ground, faces turned to each other, fear written on their expressions, as the life left their sightless eyes when they exhaled their last stinking breaths at each other.

Cord shook his head, looked down at Blue, who stood at his side, then went to gather his gear and move his camp. He soon found the tethered horses of the outlaws and brought them into camp. After securing the bodies across the saddle, he flipped the reins over the necks and slapped the horses on the rump to send them on their way, knowing they would find their way back to the familiar surroundings and the corral of other horses at the outlaw cabin. Now, maybe he could still get some sleep somewhere back in the timber and away from this mess.

13

WILLOW

CORD DID NOT THINK THERE WAS A CONCERTED EFFORT TO find him, and even if there was, he would only do what he normally would – exercise all caution as to being seen by keeping out of the open as much as possible. When he broke camp at first light, he decided to continue north, learn the lay of the land and more about the people that had moved into the territory.

He followed a game trail that kept to the trees and was high enough on the slope of the hills to afford an expansive view of the Rio Grande valley below. Where the river twisted and turned on the valley floor, the wagon road stayed below the edge of the wide alluvial fan that stretched into the valley from the big hills where Cord rode. The formation of the slope of the fan stretched far into the valley before dropping to the grassland of the valley floor. The flats of the fan were covered with mountain mahogany, greasewood, sage, gramma grass, and several different berry bushes. It was a little more than two miles before Cord broke from the timber to cross the flats toward the river. Having spotted a prospectors' camp, he wanted to visit with them and see if they had any trouble with outlaws or had heard of others being attacked.

Although Cord tried to put the memory of last night's attack from his mind, he was unsuccessful and replayed the happenings in his mind. He remembered the words of his father, *"You can't wait until your opponent makes his move. You have to learn to read him and anticipate what he might do. Whenever someone is up to no good, they usually give themselves away. Most by their eyes—they squint and they'll even move their head forward as if trying to get an advantageous view, or their eyes dart around looking to see if you're the only target or how they will escape. Their nostrils flare as they take a deep breath, readying themselves for the battle, and they'll steady their stance, maybe move their feet wider apart, drop into a bit of a crouch as if they're going to pounce on their prey, often spreading their arms wide or lifting their shoulders. Different body movements tell different stories, but if you're watchful, you'll learn and will be able to detect their intentions before they make that final and often deadly move. If you don't want to be the victim, then you must learn to anticipate what they will do before they move."* Time and again, his father's words had proven true and beneficial to Cord as he had grown and experienced the ways of the type of men that preyed on others. Such was the case last night. Cord chose not to intervene until they showed themselves and then he was ready before they were ready for him, and they were the ones that now lay over the back of their horses.

————

"Hey, Wallace! You might wanna come take a look at this!" shouted Blondy, standing in the doorway as he watched two horses trot toward the corral.

"What is it?!" growled Wallace as he stumbled to the doorway.

"Take a looksee," answered Blondy, as he nodded to the two horses. "Ain't that Spencer's blaze-face sorrel? An' that other'n looks like Snake's."

"That them o'er the saddle? Better be, otherwise I'd hafta kill 'em fer bein' so blasted stupid!"

The other men gathered near the corral as Blondy opened the gate to let the horses in with the others.

Wallace watched the horses for a moment, then started barking orders, "Dixie—you'n Johnny drop the bodies, strip the gear, and let the horses get some water an' feed. Albert—get some rope an' you'n Blondy here, drag them bodies o'er to the gulley yonder, roll 'em in and kick some o' the bank o'er 'em. Make sure they're covered. Don' wan'em stinkin' more'n they did when they was alive."

There was considerable grumbling among the men, but each one stepped to his task, knowing

Wallace was in no mood for griping or complaining. Wallace turned back to the cabin, doing his own grumbling as he re-entered the cabin and left the others to their chores. When they finished, they came inside, and Dixie went to the stove to start some bacon for breakfast. Blondy quietly grabbed the coffee pot and went outside to the little creek that dropped from the high country and chuckled its way to the gulley below. When he returned with the big enamel pot, he put it on the stove where Dixie was frying the bacon, glanced to the table where Albert Brown was making some pan biscuits for Dixie to cook after the bacon. Blondy looked at Brown, saw Johnny Barnes sitting on a bunk, elbows on knees and head down, slowly shaking it side to side. Blondy chuckled, "What's the matta' Johnny? Them bodies make you sick or sumpin'?"

"Not the bodies—it's him!" pointing to Brown, "He has never washed his hands an' now he's rollin' biscuits!"

Brown cackled, "That's seasonin' boys, seasonin'. That's why they's so good! They been seasoned right proper!" he chuckled, wiping his hands on his pants leg and returning to the task of making the biscuits with a sadistic grin at the others. "Don' like it? Don' eat 'em. Just more fer me and th'others!"

Blondy returned to the table and sat down opposite Wallace. He nodded, then asked, "Who d'ya think dunnit?" referring to the killing of the two.

"I'm thinkin' it's that same one that got the jump

on us yestiddy. Din't Spence say he thot it was the same one what broke Brady's jaw?"

"Ummhmm, but you told us all to find him. Maybe they did. They knew the tracks that man's horse made, and prob'ly jumped 'em some'eres. And it'd be just like Snake to want to find him and kill him and come back and brag about it."

"Yeah, but they ain't braggin' now and we're two men short."

"Ain't nuthin' the five of us can't handle! They weren't much help nohow," answered Blondy, leaning forward on the table as he looked at Wallace.

"Wal, you're right 'bout them not bein' much help, an' they prob'ly caused more headaches for us by gettin' found and shot up. But we can still take care o' things. There's some diggin's up the big river —a place they're callin' Willow. Ain't much, but I hear tell there's been some color found so maybe we ought to go inspect things," he chuckled as he thought of the possibilities of more prospectors with gold pouches. He knew what it was to have success at the business of robbing and killing. When he rode with his brother and the gang they had assembled, they had accumulated a good amount of money—so much so, they had to stash it in the mountains when they were fleeing the law and the soldiers under Chivington.

His brother and most of the others had been caught, taken to hang, but were killed by what they called a firing squad, and only him and two others got away. After spending a couple years down in Santa Fe and making his living as a gambler, he chose to make the big gamble and return to Colorado and eventually recover the stash made before, but that had not happened, yet. And he was biding his time, not wanting to reveal the location while there was anyone around that might suspect that his real identity was John Reynolds.

In the meantime, there were other diggings and towns starting that would make easy pickings. Willow, Eureka, San Juan City, and others that were springing up wherever there were miners, hopeful of the big strike. He had heard of those called Howardsville, Gladstone, Niegoldsville, most amounting to little more than a saloon and livery and named after the first prospector to dig a prospect hole. But wherever there were gold diggings, there were men that might have a pouch to take or more, anything to pass the time and scout the area to see if anyone was still looking for the survivors of the Reynolds gang massacre and that might know where the Reynolds treasure was buried. And if they did well and stole enough pouches to make them rich, all the better. He chuckled to himself at the thought of more than one treasure to be had.

Wallace scowled, turned back to Blondy and ordered, "You! Take one o' them," nodding toward the other men—"and backtrack them horses. An' you two..." nodding to Brown and Barnes—"go with him. We need ta' find that varmint and take his scalp!

Now! Skedaddle! Vamoose!" he shouted as he waved his arms overhead as if to scare them off. The four men did as ordered, and Blondy teamed up with Brown while Barnes sided Dixie and they rode from the cabin with Blondy in the lead. He soon motioned for Dixie to come close as he pointed to the tracks, "You're the best tracker we got. You take the lead till we find where they were kilt—then we'll split up!"

With a nod, Dixie dropped to the ground, checked the tracks for any distinguishing character-istics, swung back aboard, and took off at a trot, often leaning to the side to check the tracks of the two horses that returned with the bodies.

14

SURVEY

THE LOW SHOULDER OF THE ALLUVIAL FAN THAT LAY BELOW the higher hills to the south, dropped into the banks of the Rio Grande just opposite a long and wide draw that came from the north with a meandering creek coming from the high mountains. The presence of a couple miners camps prompted Cord to cross the river at the shallows and visit with the prospectors. When Kwitcher came from the water, stopped and rolled his hide to rid himself of the excess water, Cord dropped to the ground and let the horse and mule do their thing, Blue followed suit, and when all were back on solid ground, Cord started toward the camp, leading Kwitcher and the mule. He hailed the camp, saw the usual response with at least one man showing a shotgun as they glared at the uninvited visitor. "I'm friendly—just wanna talk!" he declared, holding his free hand high, the other trailing the animals.

"C'mon in, but be careful 'bout it!" growled the shotgunner.

Cord nodded and walked closer, taking in the work of the men. He guessed there were at least three, unusual for the time and place, but one was working a rocker box, the second shoveling gravel from the edge of the creek, and the third was standing guard. All three watched as Cord neared, "You fellas had any visitors?"

The shotgunner scowled, "Just you, why?"

"I wanted to pass the word to be careful of visitors," he chuckled, nodding to the gunner, "but I see you are already. There's been a small bunch of men, raiders, outlaws, call 'em whatever you want, but they've been hittin' claims, stealin' an' killin'. Four or five of 'em now, but there were more."

"What'chu mean, more?" growled the gunner.

"Couple of 'em tried to get me in the night, but they were belly down 'cross their saddles when they left."

The gunner let a grin split his face as he relaxed "Now, that's more like it. We'd heard 'bout them fellas an' was thinkin' they might come thisaway, but so far, you're the onliest one."

"Any diggin's further up?" asked Cord, nodding toward the mouth of the draw.

"Reckon so, don' know how many, mebbe two, three. Don't see much of any of 'em."

"If you do, pass the word. These fellas show no mercy an' would just as soon shoot as talk."

"What's yore interest?" asked one of the others.

"Oh, just don' like to see stuff like that happen. Muh daddy taught me better!" answered Cord as he swung back aboard Kwitcher.

The man at the rocker called, "What's yore handle?"

"I'm Cord Beckett, you?"

"I'm Heck Ramsey, an' that'ns,"—nodding to the one with the shovel—"John the Baptist, an' that'ns Little Joe."

Cord nodded to each one, chuckling at the names, looked to the shovel man, "John the Baptist?"

He grunted, "Yup—used to be a preacher, but it din't pay very well. Thought I'd pass the collection plate under the water and see what I'd come up with!" he grinned.

"Any luck?"

"Little, more hope than anything." He waved his arm around, "But this is the First Baptist Church of Willow! Best cathedral I ever been in." He grinned as he picked up his shovel to return to work.

Cord nodded and chuckled, "It is that!" Looking around at the tall timber that climbed the precipitous hillsides on the south and the clay and sandstone shoulders that stood proudly at the mouth of the big gulch of Willow Creek. It was beautiful country and Cord never failed to enjoy the majesty of God's creation and always gave Him the credit for the panoramic beauty. He nudged Kwitcher away from the miner's camp, retracing his tracks to the shallows crossing of the Rio Grande, and had no sooner come from the water than he got that nagging feeling that crawled up his back that forewarned him of his being followed. He stood in his stirrups and scanned the flats below the alluvial plateau, looked along the riverbanks with all its cottonwoods, aspen, and occasional spruce, yet nothing moved except the creatures on the wing. With a heavy sigh, he dropped back into his saddle and heeled Kwitcher westward to follow the Rio Grande further upstream and learn more about his territory.

The sun was high overhead when Cord, still with that crawling feeling up his spine, chose to take to the timber and make his way to a high shoulder that showed rimrock below and a small clearing on top. Thinking that would be a good promontory lookout to scan his backtrail and take a midday break, he nudged Kwitcher into the black timber to make the climb. Once at the crest of the shoulder, a grassy clearing below a cluster of aspen promised graze for the animals, and Cord dropped to the ground, stretched out the tethering rope, and with rifle in hand, binoculars hanging from his neck, he took to the clearing atop the rimrock.

Feeling the cool of the ground on his belly as he stretched out, he rose to his elbows, binoculars in hand and began his scan. His straight-line view of his backtrail was a good four miles, and he recognized the terrain above the diggings he had just visited.

Although the river initially flowed west to east in the valley bottom, below him it had bent back toward the hills and came from the west to flow north before bending back to the west. The trail he followed kept to the timberline below him and was partially hidden around the point of timbered foothills. Nothing moved, no dust showed, not even a mule deer or elk that was common in this country, had shown itself. Those creatures usually came to the river for water and graze in the early morning or early evening, and spent this time of the day in the shade of the high country timber or grazing in mountain parks with deep grasses. But he was looking for two-legged varmints, but even they had taken to the shade or something, thought Cord.

He rose to his feet and walked back to the animals to retrieve some jerky from the saddlebags and have a bit of lunch before continuing his journey. He was not ready to make camp, even though he was tempted to wait for whoever or whatever was following him. The feeling that had him on edge had never failed him before, and there was no other explanation. He rubbed behind Blue's ears as he spoke, "So fella. What'chu think? Somebody followin' us?" and rubbed the smiling dog's ears again.

———

"Looks like he crossed o'er there," declared Dixie, pointing to the riverbank at the shallows, the natural crossing of the Rio Grande at the mouth of Willow Creek. Without waiting for an answer, Dixie pushed his mount into the water and led the way across the shallows, always looking at the far bank, expecting some confrontation, but none came. As they put the river behind them, they spotted the miner's camp alongside the creek and with a wave, Dixie started toward the claim.

But his approach was halted by the shout of a man that commanded, "Stop where you are! You come any further, you're gonna hafta introduce yore-sef' to yore maker!"

Dixie reined up, stood in his stirrups to look toward the speaker, then turned back to motion the others to stop. When he turned, he called out, "We're trackin' a wanted man! You seen anybody passin' by earlier?"

"What'chu wan' him fer?" answered the one known as John the Baptist.

"He kilt some friends o' mine. We got a hangin' rope for him. We don' need fellas like him around, don'cha think?"

"Depends. Why'd he kill 'em?"

"Dunno, they just come back into camp o'er their saddles. We been trackin' him all day!" Both men were having to shout to be heard, but John was not about to let the others within easy shooting range. Dixie added, "So, you did see him, huh?"

"We saw a fella—don' know nuthin' 'bout no shootin' tho. But he ain't here, so you fellas just go on away from here and find him some'eres else--y'hear? We ain't wantin' no comp'ny!"

John put a period at the end of his sentence with a bullet from his big Sharps that boomed like a cannon and echoed across the wide draw. The horses of the visitors spooked but were held with a tight rein, and no one lost their seat.

Blondy called to Dixie, "C'mon Dixie, looks to me like that fella came an' went. Ain't those his tracks o'er yonder?" pointing to an obvious trail just a stone's throw off to the left.

Dixie stood in his stirrups, looked at the tracks, pointed to them, and called out to the miners, "That his trail? Where he left?"

"Yore the tracker! Figger it out your own self!" shouted John, waving the muzzle of his Sharps.

"Hold on! Don't go shootin' that cannon again! We're leavin'!" declared Dixie as he reined his sorrel toward the tracks, waving to the others to follow.

————

CORD STARTED to rise from his promontory when distant movement caught his eye, and he dropped to his belly and focused the field glasses on the crossing of the river below the diggings. He saw four riders come from the water, although they were too far away to recognize. But the color of the horses was familiar. A big sorrel in the lead, followed by a grey, and two bay horses. He nodded to himself, "Ummhmm, that's the bunch of Reynolds's gang, or Wallace or whatever he wants to call himself." He sat up, took a deep breath, and rose to his feet, letting his mind travel the familiar paths of planning his next move in this job of man-hunting. He had long ago determined that it was not his chosen way of life, but because of his early determination to hunt down the killers of his family, it was a way that had been forced upon him, and he had proven himself more than capable. Now he had a debt to pay to Marshal Sheffenberg, who had given him the badge and the job to make his early man-hunting legal. But the tables had turned, and now he had to face being the one that was being hunted.

15

BOX CANYON

As Cord dropped from the promontory and returned to Kwitcher and the mule, he was thinking about his father and their times together—times his father always used for teaching. One time when they were fishing, his dad cast the fly near the opposite bank and began to reel it in, slowly, and across the current, bouncing slightly on the rolling waters. As he did, he explained, *"Sometimes, what you want to catch is hiding out, like the big brown trout under that bank, and you have to cast the bait close enough for him to see, or at least near enough to bring him out in the open. Then, when he goes for the bait..."* and simultaneously with the teaching moment, a big trout hit the fly and his dad went to work reeling in the prize. When he held it on the bank, he looked at Cord and continued, *"You might not always catch your prize, but you will often bring it out of hiding and then, who knows, maybe you'll get him one way or another."*

It almost felt like he was running away, and that did not sit well with Cord. He looked around, reined up and stood in his stirrups, twisted around and looked at his back trail. He had intentionally dropped to the valley floor from the edge of the trees, leaving an obvious trail for the manhunters to follow. Nothing showed, no riders visible in the distance, yet, but it would take a while for them to ride from the last place they were seen to the bend of the river that took the Rio Grande around the low buttes where the valley had a dog-leg bend back to the west. With a glance to the sun, Cord guessed them to be a good hour or maybe two behind him. He dropped back into the seat of his saddle, looking about. Before him, the grassy bottomed valley carried the meandering Rio Grande River, while bald buttes, some with rimrock high up, shouldered in from the north side. On the south side, low-rising timber-covered foothills lay before the higher mesas and rocky-topped hills that were often split by runoff draws, showing the pale green clusters of aspen that hid in the shadows. He pushed on, determined to show his trail, but not in an obvious way to make the followers think he was aware of their following.

A few times, the Rio Grande River pushed against the western hills, crowding the trail into the trees to ride above the water until the river bent back into the valley bottom. He neared a deeper cut draw on his left that had carried runoff or floodwaters, but was now little more than a trickle and no miners showed anywhere within sight. Cord nudged Kwitcher closer as he looked for a campsite, but more importantly, a site that would offer ample cover for his defense or counter-attack. He chose to go a little further west, anticipating a better choice a little further along. Across the river and in the flats on the north side, two other creeks came from the foothills and fed the larger Rio Grande. The larger creek showed a miner's tent and the workings of a claim on the shore, but no one showed. Cord kept moving, and with another glance to the lowering sun as it was nearing the horizon before him, he spotted the shadows of what might be a deeper canyon where the Rio Grande bent back into the mountains.

———

"Now he's makin' it easy for us. I'm thinkin' he might know we're followin'," said Dixie as he stood from his close-up examination of the hoofprints of the horse, mule and dog that told of the passing of the man they hunted. Dixie turned toward the river, pointing as he spoke, "An' I think he's goin' upriver —prob'ly lookin' for a spot to ambush us, like he did Brady'n them."

"You been up thataway? You know where he might be goin'?" asked Blondy, glaring at Dixie. He was getting impatient, knowing Wallace was a short-tempered sort, and if they did not return with that man's scalp sooner than later, he'd probably be wanting their scalps.

"Mebbe – if'n it was me..."—he started, looking at the sun, shading his eyes as he looked upriver—"I think I'd be goin' to that there box canyon. Plenty places there for an ambush."

"Can you get ahead of him and ambush him?" asked Blondy, hopeful of setting a trap for the shooter that had done in their companions.

"Mebbe, 'course there ain't no way o' knowin' fer sure, but...mebbe," answered Dixie, stepping back aboard his flashy sorrel gelding with the front white stockings marking his lower legs. "If'n I take off o'er these hills—keep to the trees—move at a purty good gitalong, I might."

"Then get with it!" ordered Blondy. He motioned to the tracks before them and declared, "We can follow these good'nuff, and that'll keep him on the move. You get ahead of him, an' if you can ambush him, do it! Just make shore you get'er done. Wallace ain't gonna be happy if'n we take too long. I'm thinkin' he's got some plans 'bout a couple good jobs that'll fix things for a while, an' I ain't wantin' to miss out!"

"Me neither!" he declared, then slapped legs to the sorrel and pointed the long-legged gelding to the trees on the south side. It was obvious his plan was to take to the trees and the foothills to find a way to cut the trail before their quarry and set up an ambush.

Blondy dug heels to his mount to lead the others, Brown and Barnes, to keep on the trail behind the shooter. They did not know the man's name, nor the purpose nor reason behind his shooting of their friends, but they knew they had to catch up with him and bring his scalp back to their leader, the man calling himself Wallace.

———————

THE RIVER PUSHED Cord back into the trees to take a bit of a game trail that traversed the steeper hillside above the water, but soon dropped back near the riverbank and in the open. Now he could see in the distance, a little less than a mile ahead, where the river bent to the southwest and disappeared into the timbered foothills. *That must be where the headwaters of the Rio Grande are...seems logical. With the snowfall of the high mountains feeding the great river and making its way down south, it would have to have high country origins,* thought Cord, grinning to himself and thinking about the Almighty Creator that carved out the riverbed when He created this beautiful country.

As he neared the big bend of the river, Cord reined up and looked around. He twisted in his seat and looked behind him but saw no obvious signs of his followers, then scanned the flats before him, the far bank of the river and the land beyond, then turned his attention on the face of the hills to his left or south of the river. The sun was already nearing the horizon of the taller mountains before him, but the shoulder of the hill beside him beckoned. He frowned as he looked at the lower cover of piñon and juniper, but at the shoulder, the timber grew thick and showed an abundance of the tall lodgepole pines that grew close to one another and offered good cover. He looked over the lay of the land and chose to ride around the point and come up on the shoulder that showed a bit of a clearing just above some rimrock and appeared to be just what he wanted.

Within moments, Cord rounded the point, saw a game trail that left the riverbank and took to the trees, and offered a way to the shoulder. Once there, he stepped down, ground tying the grulla, the lead of the mule dallied around the saddle horn, and with Blue at his side and the Winchester in hand and binoculars hanging around his neck, he walked toward the trees to take a look at his back trail, thinking his followers would soon be coming within sight.

Cord dropped to his knees behind a big moss-covered boulder that sat atop the rimrock of the shoulder of the hillside. It offered a good view of the valley below, but as Cord soon noticed, it did not allow him to see very far down his backtrail. Another shoulder of the same hill pushed further into the river valley and obstructed his wider view. But he could see a good half mile of his backtrail, and there was nothing showing. A couple deer had wandered down to the river's edge for a drink and some graze and showed no sign of alarm. Cord nodded, turned back toward his campsite, and started to stand, but the whine of a bullet cut through the nearby aspen as the projectile slammed into his shoulder, spinning him around and slamming him to the ground. He remembered the whistling whine of the Whitworth sniper bullet that he had heard earlier on this venture and wondered if this was the same man. Cord clasped his rifle as he started to crawl closer to the boulder, but another whistling whine, and he felt a smashing hit to the side of his head, and everything slowed as blackness covered his eyes. He felt himself falling and reached out to catch himself, but consciousness quickly slipped away.

16

FRIENDS

IT WAS THE PAIN THAT BROUGHT HIM BACK TO consciousness. Hard, stabbing pain on the side of his head and a dull throbbing pain in his shoulder. Darkness surrounded him as he started to slowly open his eyes, just a slit, and the faintness of dull light hurt. He squinted, stifled a moan from the pain, refusing to move until he knew where he was and more. Conscious of his raspy breath, he slowed his breathing, taking shallow breaths so he would not move his chest. He felt warm, and the weight of something seemed to hold him still, but he could move his toes, his feet, however little. His fingers worked, and he felt his hands. With his eyes open just a slit, there was nothing or no one within view, but he appeared to be in something that held daylight at bay. A cave? Had he fallen into a hole or something? But no, the only pain was in his head and shoulder—if he had fallen, he would feel it in other places.

He slowly opened his eyes a little further, movement caught his attention. As he moved only his eyes to see, he saw the back of a buckskin-clad figure, but the shoulders showed beading. That would not be the outlaws, maybe...and the figure slowly stood, and he saw it was a woman, a native woman, and familiar. She turned and frowned at the still figure before her. Kneeling beside him, she reached out and smiled, "You are awake. That is good." It was the familiar voice of Lone Eagle, the shaman of the Uncompahgre Ute led by Chief Ouray, and the woman that had chosen Cord for a partner at the last Bear Dance in the early spring.

Cord frowned, asked with a raspy voice, "How'd I get here?"

"Broken Arrow brought you here. He found you when they went on a hunt in the lower valley. They heard shots nearby. Broken Arrow saw and knew your big horse, and found you near. They brought you back, and you have been sleeping for two days."

"Two days?!" asked an incredulous Cord, trying to sit up. Lone Eagle grinned and with one hand on his chest, pushed him back.

"Do not move. You have two wounds." She lightly touched his shoulder and nodded to his head, "You had a bullet in your shoulder and a bad wound on your head. It looks like a bullet tried but could not get through your hard head!" She giggled and smiled as she sat back on her heels.

Cord knew she was referring to the time they

could not agree on him leaving or staying with her, but his duties required that he fulfill the task asked of him by Marshal Sheffenberg. He sighed heavily, glanced around, "You have anything to eat? I'm starving!" he said, as he shook his head and put his hand to his shoulder, wincing. "Did you take the bullet out?" looking at his shoulder.

"Yes,"—and she reached to the side of his pillowed head and showed Cord a sizable chunk of deformed lead, "and I have been tending your wounds with my medicines."

Cord smiled, remembering her remedies, and remembering that most were much better than any of the medicines that could be purchased in a White man's store.

Lone Eagle rose to her feet and went to the entry flap, glanced back at Cord, and said, "I will be back with your food. Do not move!" she stated sternly, shaking her finger at her patient.

———

IT WAS another two days before Cord saw the sunlight and breathed fresh air. He was sitting on the willow back rest and watching the beautiful Lone Eagle as she cooked the strips of backstrap venison provided by her brother, Broken Arrow. He had visited them, checking on Cord, and explained about finding him. "We heard the shots after we saw three riders below the trees. When I saw movement in the trees, I found your horse, mule, and dog and knew you were near. We backtracked the animals, found you and saw a man coming from the trees. We believe he was the one who shot you, but he will shoot no more. He was not dead when my warriors tied him on his horse, left the arrows in him, and sent him back to the others. We watched as they took the man and quickly left the valley. Then we brought you here."

Cord was remembering the conversation as he sat watching Lone Eagle, and looked up when he saw Broken Arrow approaching. With a nod, he greeted his friend, and Broken Arrow sat opposite Cord and asked, "Do you know the one who shot you?"

"Yes. I don't know which one, but I knew the four who were following me. I was preparing to ambush them when I was shot. I guess the shooter had circled around and got ahead of me—he probably knew the area better, since I had never been here."

"You were attacked less than a half-day's ride toward the sunrise, near the big river canyon that some call a box canyon."

"I remember where I was, but I didn't know your camp was so close." Cord looked around, saw Lone Eagle getting ready to serve the food. He looked at Broken Arrow, "Those men and their leader, a man who calls himself Wallace, but I think his real name is Reynolds, are the ones causing all the trouble in this part of the country. They've been ambushing many of the prospectors, miners and such, killing, robbing, and more. I don't know the name of the one that attacked me, but I believe he had tried before. He has a special rifle for long-distance shooting, one that was used in the war." He paused, remembering the earlier attack by the man with the Whitworth sniper rifle, then continued, "My friend, the marshal, asked me to find them and bring them to justice however I choose," Cord grinned at that and looked to Lone Eagle as she brought a platter of meat, potatoes, and more to him. She also carried one for her brother, and she served them both, then returned to the fire for her own food before returning to Cord's side.

Broken Arrow watched his sister, saw her sit next to Cord and bump shoulders with him in an unusual display of affection. He lifted his eyebrows as he looked at her, showing his concern. He knew she wanted Cord for her life mate, but they had already decided they could not be together—she had to stay with her people because she was their medicine woman, and Cord had his duties as a deputy marshal for the territory. But it was not his place to intervene.

———

THEY HEARD the shots and recognized the big boom of Dixie's sniper rifle and picked up the pace, kicking their mounts to a canter. They had agreed that Dixie would take the high trail through the timber to try to get ahead of the man they were hunting and kill him if he could. Now, Blondy was hopeful their hunt was over and they could take a scalp back to Wallace. They rounded the timbered shoulder that pushed into the valley and were suddenly brought up short by a band of about ten or twelve Indians. Blondy reined up as did the others and started to reach for their rifles but the sudden shout from the leader of the Indians stopped him.

"No!" shouted the leader of the natives, holding his hand up before him. When the outlaws stopped, the warrior pulled the horse with the wounded Dixie hunkered over in the saddle alongside. "Take this man and leave this valley. This,"—he stated as he waved his arm about—"is our land and you are not wanted here. If you come again, we will kill you!" growled the leader, as he slapped the butt of the horse ridden by Dixie. Had he not been tied to the saddle, he surely would have fallen, but as the horse trotted to the others, the hulk of the wounded man wobbled precariously as he moaned and grunted, "Get me outta here!"

Blondy motioned to Barnes and said, "Grab the reins and git!" Blondy and Brown backed their horses away, swung them around, and started away at a trot and quickly picked it up to a canter to put the band of natives behind them.

When they were sure they were not followed, Dixie cried out, "Stop! Get this arrow outta me! I can't take it!"

Blondy nodded to Barnes and Brown and

ordered, "Get him down. We'll see what we can do, but we ain't wastin' any time. Them Injuns could be follerin' us and I don' wanna get muh scalp lifted!"

When they had Dixie on the ground, Barnes examined the wounds, tore the shirt away, and looked closer. He looked up at Blondy, "This'll take some doin'. We might cut off the shafts, wrap him some, but this'll take more'n we can do here!"

"Do it then! Quit wastin' time. If he makes it, alright, if'n he don't, wal, that'll be alright too."

They made camp for the night, and Barnes took over the wound tending. After some digging, moaning, and cutting, the arrows were finally freed from the wounds and the wounds were packed with pieces of Dixie's shirttail, then bound up with some torn-off pieces of his bedroll. By morning, their only concern was whether to bury him or leave him to rot, and without any other concerns, they kicked some pine needles over his body and left. With Barnes leading the sorrel that had been Dixie's pride and joy, the two men were arguing over who would get the Whitworth rifle, and Blondy solved the argument by announcing he had already claimed it.

17

HUNT

"I SENT YOU OUT TO GET THE SHOOTER AND WHAT'DYA DO? You get another'n kilt!" roared Wallace as he stood by the corral fence. The three men had returned and were sheepishly stripping the gear from their horses as Wallace roared and fussed.

"Boss, Dixie did say he shot the one we was huntin'. Said he was sure he got 'im!" answered Blondy, his saddle over his shoulder as he carried it to the fence. After flipping it onto the top rail and covering it with the blanket, he climbed atop the fence and looked down at Wallace, "Ain't that what you wanted—us to kill the shooter?"

Wallace mumbled and grumbled, shaking his head and kicking at the dirt, "Yeah, yeah," he drawled, then glared at Blondy, "But'chu weren't s'posed to get another'n kilt! We're gonna need ever' man we got an' any we can get to get done what's afore us!"

"What's the hurry? These miners ain't goin' nowhere and they ain't got no place to spend their money cep'n the trader o'er to the gap."

Blondy dropped down beside Wallace and the two walked back to the cabin, speaking in low tones that Barnes and Brown could not hear. As the two finished stripping their gear and hanging it on the fence rail, Brown asked, "You noticed we ain't been gettin' much of anything and any time we bring back a poke or such, he don't share it? This setup is beginnin' to be plumb unprofitable!"

"Ain't that the truth! But...you got any other ideas?" answered Barnes, glancing toward the cabin where Blondy and Wallace had gone.

"Hummmph, anything'd be better'n nuthin'! An' nuthin' is just what we got here!"

As the two disgruntleds started to the cabin, both Blondy and Wallace emerged, and Wallace began with, "We're gonna go back to the Gap, see what we can find 'tween here'n there, mebbe look 'round some an' if it don't look good, we might go back o'er to South Park, Fairplay, 'round there."

Barnes and Brown looked at one another, nodded slightly, and looked back to Wallace. Both men had talked before about Wallace maybe being John Reynolds and remembering the tales of buried loot by the Reynolds gang somewhere in the South Park area. Maybe things were beginning to look up for the pair, at least that was what they were both thinking as they suppressed a grin.

————————

CORD WAS FEELING BETTER, and he thought he would be alright in the saddle. He had known injury before, and here in the high country, wounds had a way of healing faster in the thin mountain air. He also knew staying in the presence of Lone Eagle any longer than was necessary would just make it harder to leave— for both of them.

The encampment of the Uncompahgre band of Ute was on the west side of the confluence of North Clear Creek and Spring Creek. The long valley of Clear Creek stretched northward and lay as a wide basin below the alluvial fans that came from the higher mountains. Spring Creek had carved its way south through a narrower valley that paralleled much of the Clear Creek Valley, but lay below the timbered flanks of high-rising buttes and flat topped mesas on the east.

Cord sat on a big moss-covered boulder beside the Clear Creek falls, where he had retreated to think and spend some time with his Lord. He enjoyed the beauty of the crystal-clear waters cascading over the edge, dropping and splashing with white water, singing the special melody of the mountains of the cascades. The sounds of the waters and the clean air of the high country allowed Cord to mentally distance himself from the present and the recent happenings that had threatened his life. He pondered the reality of eternal life that would one day be enjoyed with his Lord and Savior. But another melody brought him back to the present.

Lone Eagle had followed with an armload of his and her clothes, those that were not buckskin, and other items that needed some washing which she used as her excuse to follow. When she was especially happy, she often hummed her own melodies crafted from the combination of her people's chants and the melodies and hymns shared by Cord. She went to the edge of the waters upstream from Cord and dropped to her knees beside the clear waters, soon busy at work while Cord watched. She looked up often to see him watching and rewarded him with a broad smile.

Cord chuckled as he watched this woman, a leader among her people and the spiritual leader and medicine woman, now as humble as any other woman and tending to the chores of her and her man's needs. She knew he would be leaving soon, and she wanted to do what she could for him. They had a special relationship with one another, but it was one that, together with their other responsibilities, did not allow any long-term commitment to one another. They chose to take advantage of any opportunity to enjoy the company of one another and to learn from and help one another as necessary.

Cord lifted his eyes heavenward and quietly worded his prayer of thanksgiving and joy for the time that had been given them, but he also asked for some direction and preparation for the days to come. His time was interrupted by footsteps behind him, and he turned to see Broken Arrow, his friend and Lone Eagle's brother, approaching. As Broken Arrow nodded to the space beside Cord, he was motioned to sit down and joined his friend and the man he considered to be his brother.

"Ouray wants you to come see him when you can. He is concerned about the failure of the whites to settle the treaty and would like your counsel."

"I would be honored. Is he ready now?" responded Cord.

"He is," replied Broken Arrow, but he nodded toward Lone Eagle, "Does she expect you to stay?"

"No, she knows I will leave soon, and she wanted to do that for me."

With a nod, Broken Arrow arose, followed by Cord, and the two men started back to the camp. Broken Arrow led the way as they walked through the village to the center, where the lodge of the chief sat near the central circle. The stoic chief sat beside his lodge, watching his woman at the cookfire, and he was working on a quiver for his arrows. He looked up as the two approached, setting the quiver aside and motioning to the blanket at his side for the men to join him.

Cord spoke first, "Broken Arrow said you wanted to see me?"

"Yes," he began, but paused for the two to make themselves comfortable, then continued, "My people tell me of many camps of White men in our land. This land," he began, motioning to the hills and valley beyond, "is our land. My people were here long before any White man ever appeared, and at the last treaty meet, it was agreed by your people that all the land west of those mountains,"—nodding to the long line of Rocky Mountains—"would be our land forever. But now those that dig for their gold come as they will and do not obey the word of your leaders."

The conversation continued through the morning, and Cord explained to the chief about his own mission. "I started out to explore this part of the country to get to know the land but also the people. I want to know where the gold hunters are and who is causing all the trouble." He had previously explained about the mission given him by Marshal Sheffenberg. "But that will also tell me how many White men there are that have come into the land of the Uncompahgre or Weeminuche. We know they are here against the treaty and it is up to the soldiers to get them to leave, but if I know where they are and how many, I can report that to the authorities as well."

"Will they listen to your words?" asked Ouray.

"That I do not know, chief. But I will try to get them to listen and to enforce the treaty. What they have allowed is not right for your people, and it is also bad for the whites. There are many that are not honorable and seek to rob the others that are trying to make their way alone. These are the ones that I seek and will bring to justice, but the others? They are not breaking the White man's law, even though they are breaking the treaty terms. I will do what I can."

"It is good. Now, go to your woman, and make your journey and return to us when you can," directed a normally very stoic chief, but he glanced up to see Lone Eagle coming toward them and he chuckled, and added, "If you can!" with a nod toward Lone Eagle.

Lone Eagle had prepared a meal of fresh venison steaks and onions, carrots, potatos, and biscuitroot. She had also prepared a side dish of service berries, elderberries, blackberries, and raspberries. When they finished and Cord sat back against the willow backrest, he smiled at Lone Eagle, "That was a very good meal, thank you."

Lone Eagle dropped her eyes, sighed heavily, "I know you are ready to leave, and I want you to know you are always here,"—she put her closed fist to her heart—"with me. Please do not wait so long to return."

Cord rose, stood before her and said, "I will do what I can as often as I can. I miss being here with you also, but..." he shrugged, and without words and only his expression, said what they both understood. She pointed to the side of her lodge where Kwitcher stood, already saddled and ready to go, with the mule's lead line dallied around the saddle horn. Blue lay beside the lodge and lifted his head and mournful eyes to Cord as he stepped near and swung aboard his saddle. With a nod to Lone Eagle, Cord rode from the camp.

18

ROUNDABOUT

Cord was pensive and reflective after he rode from the village of the Ute. He believed the activity of the gang of Wallace would be somewhat curtailed, what with losing another of their number, and he thought they believed him dead. He chose to take this opportunity to further explore the district that was now his assigned territory and get to know the land and the people as well as understand the number of White settlers and miners that had infiltrated the territory of the Ute.

As usual, after spending time with Lone Eagle, Cord's emotions were stirred, but he chose to put that behind him and focus on his current situation. He knew that Wallace and his bunch would not be the only outlaw types that would be trying to make their fortune in what they considered to be the easy way, by taking it from others. Yet he also knew there were more that were honest and hard-working types that just wanted to make their fortune and maybe provide for their family. Even the Reynolds brothers had at one time been honest citizens and become soldiers for their cause, but circumstances changed and opportunities intervened and their lives had taken a wrong turn. Cord knew that could have just as easily happened to him, after seeing his family murdered by the Red Legs under the guise of the war. But he reflected on the many times his father had taken him aside, whether to the woods to hunt or fish, or on a walk about just to have time together and to teach. Cord was thankful for such times for not only did he learn more about God and His Word, he had also committed himself to serving God in his own way, no matter the circumstances. When he accepted Christ as his Savior at his father's side while they sat on a log in the woods, he reflected on what his father taught about the need of every person to come to an awareness of his need of a Savior.

"Son, you see, the Bible teaches that all are sinners," he began, as he pointed to the scripture before him, *Romans 3:23. " Now, He adds in 5:12, and 6:23 that because of that sin, the penalty is death. Now, that doesn't just mean we will die, because everyone will die. What that means is that penalty is death and hell forever, or to spend eternity in the oblivion of Hell. But..."* and his father put his arm around Cord's shoulders and drew him near, *"God loved us so much, He does not want us to have to pay that price. So, he sent his own son, the Lord*

Jesus, to pay that terrible price for us – and He did that
when He died on the cross for us. That's why 6:23 says, ...
the wages of sin is death; but the gift of God is eternal life
through Jesus Christ our Lord. See, it's a gift. But just like
any other gift, it has to be received. And you do that by
prayer, and asking God for that gift of eternal life."

CORD SMILED at the memory when he bowed his head
with his father and prayed a simple prayer where
Cord admitted he was a sinner, and that the penalty
for sin was death, but he wanted to accept the gift of
eternal life bought and paid for by Jesus. And when
he did, his life changed completely.

As he remembered that, he also reflected on
thinking how good it would be if he could tell all the
'bad people' about Jesus and maybe they wouldn't be
bad anymore. Cord chuckled to himself, remembering times when that had been true, but he also
acknowledged that there are many that would never
accept that gift of eternal life, choosing instead to do
their own thing and rob, steal, and kill, believing
they could do so without fear of any consequences.
But he also remembered his father saying, *"Some-*
times, God will use us to teach others not just about the
love of God, but also about the consequences."

Cord had spent his time recuperating, learning
from Broken Arrow about the country around them.
Broken Arrow had told of trails, wagon roads, and
more, and now Cord was following a trail he had

learned about from Broken Arrow. He had followed Spring Creek north, crossed over a low saddle between mountains at the head of the creek and continued on to another crossing he had referred to as Slumgullion pass. Broken Arrow said he heard some White men refer to a land formation beyond the pass by the same name and they had called it a pass. "It is where the side of the mountain had slid down, taking trees and more, dammed up the river and made a lake," explained Broken Arrow.

Cord sat his horse, looking at the strange land mass that was surrounded by standing trees, but bald on the face of the slide, showing earth in tones of yellow, orange, and pale shades of both colors. The trees at the foot of the slide stood at odd angles, obviously pushed by the movement of the soil. The hills around the slide were spotted with clusters of aspen that whispered with their leaves in the breeze, baring their white-barked souls, yet standing firm and tall to add color to the mountainside. Beyond the slide, a long lake stretched into the canyon of the Grand River, and Cord knew that to be Lake San Cristobal, named by the early Spanish explorers.

Cord looked down the valley that made a bit of an *S* twist as the Grand River worked its way from the high country north. Cord nudged Kwitcher onto the trail that sided the river, making its way through the tall spruce and towering lodgepole pines, twisting through the thickets of aspen that whispered with their leaves as they passed. Cord spotted a few prospect holes, the ever-present reminders of the invasion of the mountains by gold seekers, but it was not until the valley bent to the northwest that he spotted the first prospector camp. Two men were busy at their work with a sluice box and a pile of fresh diggings. A little further upstream, another man was on his knee beside the water, using a wide pan to wash samples, searching for fresh sign of gold. Cord's hail caught them by surprise, and the man with the shovel quickly replaced the spade with a shotgun as he hollered out, "Hold it right thar! Don' come no closer less'n you wanna spring a leak!"

Cord chuckled, lifted his hands, and nudged Kwitcher closer, guiding him with his knee pressure. "Whoa boy," muttered Cord as he neared, just loud enough for his horse to hear and the big grulla stopped, head lifted, ears forward, and the mule moved alongside. "I'm friendly, just wanna talk."

"Step on down, keep yore hands high!" answered the shotgunner.

The river twisted around from above and dropped over a narrow falls, the sound of the waterfalls only slightly muffled by the nearby trees. A gravel bank pushed into the shallows, and the man beside the sluice box leaned on the box, keeping it between himself and the visitor. A thicket of aspen stood tall behind them, and Cord spoke, "I came from o'er the mountains, down by Wagon Wheel Gap. There's been some trouble by a gang of outlaws —killin' and robbin' prospectors—and I was wonderin' if you fellas had seen any of that or if everything is goin' alright for you."

"What's it yore bizness?" asked the shotgunner, a pot-bellied, whiskery-faced, just past middle age, grumpy sort.

Cord put his hand to his vest pocket, but stopped at the command of the shotgunner. "Hold it! What'chu reachin' for?"

"You asked why it was my business—I'll show you, if it's all right?"

"Go 'head on—but easy now!"

Cord withdrew his badge, held it in his palm as the men craned to look at the brass six-pointed star with a circle in the middle that held the words, *Deputy US Marshal.*

"A marshal!? Wal', why'nt ya say so!"

"I think I just did," answered a grinning Cord.

The talker lowered his shotgun and asked, "So, you got a name whut goes wit' that thar' badge?"

Cord nodded, "Cordell Beckett, you?"

"I'se called Shoofly! Shoofly Jones! And that thar,"—pointing with his chin to the man beside the sluice box—"is Mac...Mac McGillicutty. Most folks cain't say his last name, so's they just calls him Mac."

The sluice box leaner nodded, gave a slight wave, and turned back to his work. Cord asked, "Many others downstream?"

"Thar's a few, most done moved on to try their luck elsewheres."

"I'm going to head over the mountains, have a

looksee yonder and pass the word thataway. I'd appreciate if you would do the same with those fellas downstream."

"Wal..." began Shoofly, rubbing his chin whiskers, "I reckon we can do that, soon'rn later. Ain't gonna take any muh time away from muh work, but if'n theys come thisaway, we'll pass the word."

Cord slowly shook his head as he grinned, "Alright then, reckon I'll just keep movin'," as he stepped back beside Kwitcher and swung aboard. He leaned forward on his pommel and looked at Shoofly, "What's the best way to get o'er them mountains," nodding to the line of towering peaks behind him.

Shoofly grinned, waved his hand to the south-west, "Just foller that trail 'long them foothills. It'll take you 'round Sunshine Peak—that's the big'un what catches the sunshine in the mornin' 'fore the others. That trail'll take you 'tween it an' another'n that's 'bout as big, then o'er the littler ones an' it'll drop you into the Animas River gorge. Then if'n you're mountain man 'nuff, you can foller it out." He paused and said, "If'n you don' already know it, the Animas River's real name is *Rio de las Animas Perdidas!*" He chuckled, "That means the River of Lost Souls! So, be careful you don' become one of 'em!" He started to turn away, then asked, "Say there, young'un. If'n we need to get aholt o' the law, how we go 'bout it?"

"Try to send word down to Wagon Wheel Gap.

There's a trader there by the name of Toots. I'll keep in touch with him as much as possible and he'll pass the word along."

The miner grinned, showing tobacco-stained teeth, what there were, and grinned as he nodded a goodbye to Cord. Cord waved over his shoulder as he turned to Blue and motioned him back to the trail. He pushed through the trees to return to the trail that fell from the natural dam of the big lake to take the high road into the thicker timber on the high side, or west side of the steep timber-covered hills that pushed the toes of their slopes into the icy waters of the high country Lake San Cristobal.

19

DISCOVERY

THREE DAYS, COUNTING HIS FIRST DAY BEFORE HE MET UP with Shoofly and friends, of travel through some of the most challenging and beautiful country Cord had ever seen, gave him time to reflect, consider, enjoy, and appreciate all that he had seen and experienced. But he also had a lot of time to look inward and realized he had made no plans for his future, his life in general, and what he wanted to do or become. His father had often encouraged him to take time to consider his actions and his plans. *"We never know what tomorrow will hold, but it is good to at least consider. Proverbs 27:1 says, Boast not thyself of tomorrow, for thou knowest not what a day may bring forth. And that simply tells us our plans are all subject to change, but that does not mean we should not plan. As my father used to tell me, 'If you aim at nothing, you'll hit it every time!'"* And as Cord remembered his father's words, he chuckled and realized he had been aiming at nothing. For several years, his thoughts had been consumed with seeking out those that had murdered his family, and since that time, he had focused on other lawbreakers and had given little thought to his own life and future.

As he rode, his eyes wandered over the steep mountainsides, the granite-tipped peaks that cradled glaciers in the many crevices and steep draws, and the wild animals that populated this beautiful creation of an Almighty God. He had a glimpse of the white coated mountain goats as the kids gamboled about the rugged cliffs. He had watched the big horn sheep contest one another as they butted heads, reminding him of many times he felt just like that. The magnificent elk with their drape of dark brown that hung around their tawny-coated shoulders and back, and the massive antlers that when mature, would stretch the full length of their bodies, with the last tip sometimes used to scratch their own rumps. These and others always caused him to give the glory to the Creator of such beauty and magnificence, but those thoughts also brought him back to the emptiness of his own future.

He broke from the trees and spotted a broken-down log cabin, the sod roof caved in, and the door ajar, hanging from one leather hinge, and he could not help but wonder who it was that built that cabin and what dreams did he have when he came to this wild land. He moved across the small park, spotted a big naked snag of a tree that had at one time risen high above and whose crown of green had touched the blue of the sky, but now was a bare skeleton of grey and blackened wood, bare branches reaching out to touch nothing, bent at the ends where age and the elements had broken the ends, and a couple turkey buzzards that sat atop watching with hungry eyes, hunkered over and moving not at all with nothing that moved below escaping their sentry, as if they somehow knew that whatever passed below would soon be their dinner.

He came to a wide basin, and the trail rode a shoulder below some steep calcite talus slopes before bending to the west and climbing over a saddle crossing to drop into a wide green basin that lay below a small snow melt pond. The cold wind whispered off the steep peaks that surrounded the basin, each holding its own glaciers and pockets of last winter's snow, adding to the chill of the high country. Cord looked through the cut between mountains to see a myriad of granite peaks stacked upon one another and stretching further west. The lowering sun was threatening to shut off the day's supply of warmth soon, and Cord nudged Kwitcher on the trail that sided a creek that Shoofly had told him about, called Cinnamon Creek, because it was the color of that favored spice, probably because of the rocks and minerals that it sprang from before cutting its way to the river below. Although the trail kept to the high side and rounded the bald face of the big mountain, Cord nudged Kwitcher to the trees on a low shoulder that sided the steep falling creek and pointed to the river valley below. He found a flat spot in the trees, decided it would make a good camp, even though he was still high up, and began making camp.

With the coals of his cook fire beside him, and Blue behind him, his blankets over the top, he snuggled down for the night. But the cold from the still-frozen ground soon seeped through the ground cover, and a chill set in, bringing him upright to feed more fuel to the fire. He looked around at the black, shadowed trees that moved slowly with the mountain breeze as if they were dancing to a tune only they could hear. A low howl came from the canyon below, and the horse and mule lifted heads as they recognized the lonesome howl of a timber wolf that was on the prowl and sang his song of hunger. Blue moved against Cord's leg, and Cord reached to pull the rifle close. Dark clouds were snagged on the silhouetted peaks while the last sliver of moon shone futile light from behind the billows.

What had been endless and magnificent beauty as he traveled through the wonders of God's creation, had now become a fearful and even terrifying blackness. Cord remembered the verse in John 3:19—*And this is the condemnation, that light is come into the world, and men loved darkness rather than light, because their deeds were evil*. He shivered with the cold but reminded himself that he knew the Light of the World who was Jesus, and he was here to represent his Savior, and he lifted his eyes heavenward and asked, "All right Lord, I don't know why all of a sudden I'm unsettled, but I'm dependin' on you."

But even though he had spoken softly, he was startled when a low growl came from behind him, and another off to his left, away from the horse and mule, but all his animals stiffened and stared at the black blanket of darkness that hung from the trees. Cord tossed another small log on the fire, causing sparks to rise into the treetops and the fire to flare. Eyes showed under the low branches of the big fir to his left, and movement behind him caused him to turn and see more eyes shining in the dark. Low growls accompanied the movements, and Cord jacked a round into his Winchester, dropped his hand to his still holstered Remington Army pistol for reassurance, and lifted the Winchester as he shouted, "Heeyawww!"

But the shout just prompted the big wolf to spring into action, and he sprang toward Cord, but the rifle blasted and bucked as Cord fired, jacked another round, and fired again, both bullets striking black fur as it leaped high, teeth bared, eyes blazing. Cord saw slobbers fall from the fangs and tongue, saw the extended paws, before he threw himself aside to cause the wounded wolf to drop almost atop Blue. But Blue was ready, teeth bared and as the black furred beast neared, Blue's teeth dug deep in the throat of the beast, bringing it to the ground, growls filling the air until an otherworldly scream came from the beast as Blue ripped back and forth, tearing the fur and hide from the beast's throat.

Cord had thrown himself aside, but toward the second of the wolves, and the more hesitant wild canine lunged toward Cord, yellow teeth bared, eyes dancing with fire. Cord rolled to the side, drawing and cocking his pistol, to meet the beast with flame stabbing from the muzzle of his pistol. The weight of the wolf drove Cord to the ground and he felt the hot slobbers on his face. In his determination and fear, Cord cocked the pistol, shoved against the thick fur of the beast's chest, and dropped the hammer again. The bullet drove into the chest, fire stabbing from the muzzle and burning hair, the stench choking Cord, but he scrambled from under the now entangled pile of canines. He rolled aside, searching for any movement other than that of Blue as he stood with front feet atop the carcass of the wolf and blood dripping from his teeth.

A quick look showed Cord that both wolves were dead, but he quickly glanced to the horse and mule, saw them nervously shifting side to side, but glaring at the trees on the far side of the clearing. More eyes shone in the darkness, reflecting the light of the fire, and Cord grabbed more wood, tossing it on the fire, always keeping his pistol at the ready as he moved. The flames climbed higher, now illuminating the trees and sparks climbing to the tree tops, and Cord holstered his pistol and grabbed his rifle and he moved with his back to the fire, watching the perimeter of the camp, searching for more flashing eyes.

He did his best to preserve his night vision, but everything was happening so fast, he had to search the edge of the trees. He thought he saw more and lifted his rifle, aimed where he had seen the eyes, and fired. Again, flame stabbed the night and the blast of the rifle echoed across the canyon walls, but he was rewarded with a whimper and another growl. Cord kept on the move, searching the darkness, watching the horse and mule for their signs of alarm, and still he moved. Suddenly the horse and mule screamed and brayed and lunged forward, but lifted their heels and kicked, the mule more effectively than the horse, but both were fighting off the attack. Cord moved closer, searching for a shot, but the mule was moving so many ways and so fast he could not shoot. But he looked to Kwitcher and saw a mass of black atop the horse's back, teeth bared and grabbing for the horse's neck. Cord ran closer, jammed the muzzle of the rifle against the wolf's neck, and dropped the hammer. The rifle roared, the horse bucked, the wolf screamed, and blood flew, but the beast had lost his grip and tumbled off only to land in a heap that Kwitcher drove his front hooves into, time and time again, screaming as he delivered the sentence of the equine court of judgment.

The mule moved about nervously as did Kwitcher but both sought the closeness of the other, and Cord stepped closer, stroking the neck and face of

Kwitcher and the neck of the mule. Blue had come close and rubbed himself against Cord's leg and the cluster of friends, four-legged and two, reveled in the presence of their longtime trail companions. It took a while for them all to settle down, and Cord dragged the carcasses of the wolves back into the timber, but the stench of blood and death remained, and with a glance to the thin grey line of early morning, Cord decided to break camp and put this all behind them.

20

CIRCUIT

DARKNESS HUNG HEAVY OVER THE STEEP-SIDED CANYON. Every footfall of the horse and mule seemed to echo before and behind them. The moon and rising sun fought for dominance, neither giving much light in the bottom of the gorge, but Cord and the animals were accustomed to traveling in the darkness, and there was enough grey light of early morning to give them confidence in the narrow trail they followed. The crashing of the waters of the Animas River provided the music as the footfalls gave the rhythmic beat to the orchestra of the high country. Cord grinned at the thought, lifting his eyes to the sheer faces of the towering peaks, many rising more than two miles high. Dropping his eyes to the bottom of the gorge, he frowned as the crashing of the rapids was momentarily muted, and he saw where an avalanche had dropped deep snows to temporarily act as a dam for the river, but the stubborn flow of water had carved its own tunnel through the deep snow, now covered with a layer of granite dust, and exit further below. It was a warning and a reminder to the traveler that death hung overhead and could come crashing down any moment, whether in the form of an avalanche of long-held ice and snow, or a rockslide loosed by constant wearing away by the elements.

He realized he was holding his breath as he lifted his eyes to scan the steep talus slopes and cliff faces, then shook his head and grinned as he breathed deep and nudged Kwitcher to a little bit quicker step. They had come about four miles since their encounter with the wolves and the canyon opened a bit wider to admit another fork of the river to fall from the western peaks. Higher up the talus slope on the west face, the dirt and rocks showed a tawny color, and lower on the slope, several prospect holes told of gold seekers. The trail entered a thicket of lodgepole pine and fir, then quickly broke from the trees, and Cord saw a cabin set back on the back of the tributary creek, and a sluice box set-up near the Animas River waters. Two men were working the sluice and the gravel thereabouts, and both were surprised when Cord called out, "Hello, the camp!"

Both men scampered about, grabbing rifles and taking cover behind the sluice box. Cord chuckled and sat still watching, then called out again, just loud enough to be heard over the waters of the river, "Don't shoot! I'm friendly and I'm comin' in!" He nudged Kwitcher forward, and Blue led the way as they neared the prospectors. Cord had his free hand held high, palm forward and open, and nodded as he neared.

"Howdy fellas. Doin' any good?"

"Whatsit to ya?" growled the bigger of the two men. Both men had the typical look of the high country prospector, whiskers, haggard clothes and looks, but the gear was well put-together, and their tools well kept.

"Oh, nuthin', just makin' talk. Been here long?" asked Cord.

"Long 'nuff, why?"

Cord shook his head, chuckled lightly, "Well, I see you're not in the mood for comp'ny, so...I'll just be movin' on. By the way, there's been some outlaws hittin' miners camps back o'er the hills yonder way, had anything like that happen round here?"

The bigger man grunted, shaking his head and waving the muzzle of his rifle around, motioning Cord to move along.

Cord said, "I understand a fella by the name of Charles Baker had found some gold along 'bout here, but that was a few years back. He got run off by the Ute. Oh, and by the way, the Ute are still around, and they still see this as their land. And...technically, it still is, according to their treaty, so you might wanna keep that in mind. You greet them like you did me, you might end up losing your hair."

Cord chuckled, nudged Kwitcher back to the trail

that crossed the shallows of the river, and took to the east bank of the river and Cord knew better than to try to make his own way in this kind of country. Shoofly had told him about Baker's Park that was about another seven or eight miles down the trail. With a glance to the sky, Cord guessed they would be there about time for a mid-day break and that would give him time to have a good look around. He supposed there would be some gold seekers busy at the riverside, but there might be other things stirring as well. He shrugged, acknowledging to himself that this trip was all about getting to know the lay of the land and get acquainted with as many people as possible.

After crossing back over the river to the north-west side, the trail hugged the steep talus slopes and offered Cord many glimpses into the woods on the other side of the river. There was sign of some earlier diggings and prospecting, but no inhabited camps or residents of the two old cabins he passed. As the valley began to open wide, he came upon another miners camp and received a better welcome. The miners offered to share their meal with Cord and bid him step down. "Ain't ver' often we get vistors roun'chere," stated the runt of the litter, a short pot-bellied man that seemed to strut when he walked, but his grin split his whiskers as he offered his hand to Cord, "I'm called Shorty! You'd think some o' these fellas could come up with a better nickname, but I've answered to that most o' my life, so..." he shrugged as he grinned. He pointed to one of the other men, "That'ns called Digger, cuz that's what he's allus doin', and," he nodded to the third man—"that's Jonesy." Jonesy was a big man, a former slave, who stood about and handbreadth over six feet, and appeared to weigh about seventeen stone, or well over two hundred pounds. His shirt was sleeveless and only two buttons struggled to hold it together below his broad chest, and even though the temperature was barely over sixty degrees, the man was shiny with sweat. He nodded to Cord, smiled broadly, and responded in a deep bass voice that sounded like it came from a deep well, "That's me. Don' know what muh real name mighta been, but been answerin' to Jonesy since I was this high," he chuckled when he held out his hand to indicate about waist high.

"Wal you'ns better come an' get it! An' you best beat Jonesy to the goods cuz if'n you don't there won' be any left!" shouted Shorty as he grinned at the others. He motioned to the big pot that hung over the cookfire, pointed to the stack of tin plates and cups, and bent to lift the big enamel coffee pot to pour the cups full of thick black coffee. He chuckled as he looked at a wide-eyed Cord when he poured his cup full, "Ahh, we don' never wash the pot. We just adds more grounds and water, set it to boilin' and pour it out. Gets a mite strong, but it'll keep ya' goin'!" he cackled.

As they finished up their meal, Cord began to

explain, "I'm the deputy marshal for this the third district. I'm makin' the rounds, getting acquainted and lettin' folks know where I can be found. That'll be o'er to Wagon Wheel Gap, there's a fella there that put in a general store and such, goes by Toots Monroe. I'll leave word with him whenever I'm out on rounds or such."

The three men sat silent and still until Shorty said, "Ain't never had no lawman visit, din't even know there's was one o' you 'round'chere. But it's good to know."

"Well, I was making my rounds sort of incognito, you know, on the quiet. But I had a change of mind, thought it might be best if folks knew I was a deputy and could be found easy enough."

"So, you been havin' any trouble?" asked Shorty, with a glance to his partners.

"There's been some. There's a bunch down near the gap that's been robbin' and killin' some of the prospectors, but since they lost a few of their men, I'm thinkin' they might leave the area—leastwise, that's what I'm hopin'," explained Cord.

"You the one what done it? You know, caused 'em to lose some men?" asked Jonesy.

"Ummhmm," nodded Cord, bracing himself for another sip of the black brew. He stood, sat the plate and cup aside, looked at the men, "Thanks for the meal and comp'ny. I'll be moseyin' on for now, but I'll stop by next time I'm around this way."

———

THE ANIMAS RIVER pushed against the steep timber-covered hills on the east, and the trail rode a slight shoulder on the west bank of the river. The valley slowly opened wide as the broad shoulders of the massive mountains shrugged back, offering fertile flatlands across the valley floor that was almost a mile wide and close to five miles long. It was a refreshing sight and Cord stood in his stirrups and stretched, twisting his torso, and taking deep breaths of the high mountain air, thin though it was, but he felt a new freedom with room to stretch and more. He noticed a newer cabin set back from the riverbank and standing in the shadows of a cluster of big spruce and fir. But the most unusual part of the sight was a woman in her long dress, a ruffled apron over the front, as she watered a flower garden in front of the cabin. Off to the side, the green stalks of corn were stretching about waist high, and the promise of other vegetables showing green in rows standing in dark soil. Beyond the cabin, the skeleton of what appeared to be the making of a barn stood tall, and beyond the barn, a man with sleeves rolled up, big hands holding long reins of a powerful team of mules, was encouraging the mules to dig deep and pull hard as they struggled to pull out a stump. It was obvious the man was clearing a field for planting, but it would probably take the rest of the summer to get enough cleared to call it a field.

Cord nudged Kwitcher toward the man, and as he neared he hailed the man, "Howdy friend!" and stopped, with his free hand held high and watched the worker halt the team and turn to look at Cord. Cord noticed the man had a pistol tucked into his waistband, and his hand dropped to the butt of the pistol as he turned to face Cord.

"Howdy!"

Cord nodded, asked, "Alright if I come closer?"

"Come'head on!" responded the man as he pulled a neckerchief from his pocket and wiped his sweat-covered brow and neck.

"Looks like you've been doin' a lotta work around here," suggested Cord, as he waved his hand about, "It's unusual to see someone actually doing something constructive. Looks like you'll have a good farm here, if you can get much to grow at this altitude. Where 'bouts you from?"

"We came from Pennsylvania. Heard about this part of the country and thought it would be a good place to make a home, grow things that all these gold-hungry miners would be willing to pay premium prices for, you know, vegetables and such. We've got a couple milk cows and some chickens, so we'll be able to offer eggs, milk, and more."

"Just the thought of fresh eggs and milk makes my mouth water," answered a grinning Cord. "Sounds to me like you'll be the one to strike it rich!"

The man grinned, chuckled, "Don' know 'bout

rich, but should make a decent living to raise a family."

The thought of a home and family struck a familiar note with Cord. He had thought that before when he settled in Oro City. He and his wife wanted to have a home and family, but she died giving birth to their stillborn infant. He shook his head at the thought, trying to put the memory aside and looked at the man, "I'm Cordell Beckett, deputy marshal for this district, just passing through. Everything goin' alright for you and the missus?"

"It is—so far. I'm Shamus McTavish, and my wife is Madelaine. You're welcome to stop by anytime, Marshal. I'm sure the wife would be glad to have a different face to look at and someone that could talk 'bout more'n just crops, dirt, and rocks and such," he chuckled and turned to resume his work.

Cord nodded, "Good to meet you, Shamus. And I just might do that next time around," and with a wave, Cord nudged Kwitcher back to the trail.

21

RETURN

THE TRAIL LEFT BAKER'S PARK BEHIND AS IT BENT WEST AS if to follow Mineral Creek, but instead it climbed the face of what was known as Sultan Mountain, a name that was given because of the shape of the peak of the mountain that resembled the headdress of the Ottoman Turks and had been given by a man that was said to have traveled that country. Cord chuckled at the thought of some sultan from the Ottoman Empire traveling this country, especially in the winter. But as he chuckled, the wagon trail, if it could be called that, made a switchback and started on the narrow shelf road across the face of the steep mountain. With the trail in some places so narrow that if anyone was driving a wagon, they would have to hug the hillside to keep the outside wheels on the road, but even so, Cord kept Kwitcher and the mule close to the face of the hills.

After no more than a couple miles, the trail bent

into the mouth of a narrow gulch where Cord was greeted by a lone prospector, riding a rawboned horse and trailing a pair of loaded burros. The man had stopped, stepped down, and hailed Cord, "Howdy, friend!"

Cord grinned, reined up, and leaned on his pommel as he answered the man, "Howdy! You alright? Havin' trouble?"

"Nah, no trouble, jus' wanta put that thar sign back up. Looks like it done fell o'er or else sumpin' or somebody knocked it o'er," he talked as he walked around his animals and bent to lift a sign that was nailed to a post of sorts. The man stood it up, wiped off the dirt to reveal the words, *Deadwood Gulch*. He chuckled as he stood it up, stacked some rocks around the base of the post, and stood back to admire his work. He dusted off his hands as he said, "Thar—that'll do!" He turned to look at Cord, "Made that sign muh own self, 'bout a year back. I'se the one what named it!"

"Why Deadwood?"

"Cuz anything that tries to go up thar will be as dead as deadwood! Heheheee!" he chuckled, his ample belly bouncing as he did. "Say, you headin' south?"

"I am."

"How's 'bout us'ns travelin' together? I sometimes get a lil' lonesome, need somebody to talk to, or listen...one 'rtuther."

"Suits me," answered a grinning Cord. "You ready to travel now?"

"Yup!" answered the prospector as he grabbed the stirrup to turn it toward his foot as he hopped on the other. The horse turned his head to look at the man, and Cord was certain the animal rolled his eyes at the sight.

As he settled into his seat, the prospector said, "By the way, I'se called Shill!" "Shill?" asked a frowning Cord.

"Aye laddie, tis short for Shillelagh!" he declared as he lifted his blackthorn walking stick from the loop at his saddle's pommel. It was the typical stick used for walking and fighting among the Irish. "But me name is Liam O'Connor, that's O'Connor that comes from the Gaelic O Conchubhair, which tells of our history as patrons of warriors –" he lifted the shillelagh and added, "and this has been passed down for three generations!" he chuckled, "Aye, though I have not been called by O'Connor for more'n a coon's age!"

Cord noticed the man's vernacular had changed from the typical rough and uneducated miner to the typical brogue of the Irish. He grinned at his company and asked, "So, you want me to call you Shill or Liam or Irish?"

"Ah, call me what'chu will, just don' call me late for dinner!" he laughed as he slapped his legs to the bony sides of his mount to catch up with Cord.

Although Liam had traveled this way before, Cord took the lead on the oft times precarious mountain trail that hugged the flanks of the San Juan Mountains and showed little sign of recent travel. They crossed over a low ridge that Liam called *Molas Pass* and dropped beside a creek that pointed them southward and down-hill. An earlier trail had sided the creek but was rerouted by a rockslide that took the trail along the western hillside before switching back south to follow what Liam called Lime Creek. Liam said, "That trail yonder follows the creek, but it gets a mite scary further down an' often gets washed out. There's another'n that takes off thataway," pointing to the timbered shoulders on the west side of the deep valley. "Let me take the lead, I wanna show you somethin' 'bout this country."

Cord waved him past and as the talkative Irishman led the way, he often turned around in his saddle to look back toward Cord and point out the sights along the way. They had gone a short distance when he said, "Now, turn around and lookee yonder," pointing to the hills behind them. "Ain't that somethin'? Looks like the good Lord just laid a stack o' griddle cakes one atop another till He made that there mountain!"

Cord looked where Liam pointed and was amazed at the strange formation of the mountain-side that did indeed look like stacks or layers, not griddle cakes, but rocks. Line upon line and layer upon layer with random brush and greenery to accent each layer. Cord shook his head and turned back to Liam, "Does everything you see remind you of food?"

"Only when I'm hungry!" cackled the Irishman. "An' since you mentioned that, how soon we gonna be stoppin' for supper?"

The sun had already passed the top of the western peaks, and the shadows were growing long in the valley as Cord looked about. He pulled out his pocket watch that told him it was nearing six, and with a glance to the sky, he asked, "How soon we gonna find a place to make camp?"

"Oh, mebbe an hour or two—that suit?"

"It does. I could use some hot coffee and some sleep," replied Cord.

"Coffee?! I'm thinkin' somethin' to eat! How 'bout some bacon, biscuits, gravy, and whatever else we find?"

"Sounds good to me, you cookin'?" called Cord.

Grumbles came from the now hunched over Liam as he slapped legs to his slow-moving horse. Cord heard something that resembled *lazy, slow, and stubborn* and he wasn't sure if Liam was talking about his horse, the donkeys, or himself.

———

WHEN FIRST LIGHT stretched the shadows before them, Cord and Liam were on the trail. The night's camp had been a cold one with wind coming off the towering peaks and their snow-filled crevasses, and it took little encouragement for them to roust out, stoke up the fire, have some hot coffee and leftover biscuits and bacon, and hit the trail. As they came to another creek in the bottom of a long valley, Liam said, "This hyar's what some call Cascade Creek, it drops down into that valley or gorge yonder, but thankfully, the trail stays high. We'll be riding 'long the bottom of a long stretch of limestone rimrock cliffs that only have scattered aspen below 'em. Up top, I went there one time, never again, ain't much o' nuthin' but gullies, rocks, trees, and rough country."

"Any settlements further on?" asked Cord.

"Ain't nuthin' you'd call settlements, but there's some gold camps, hot springs, diggin's and such all along there. Even some fools that went up into the canyon lookin', but ain't nuthin' there."

It was late morning when Cord caught a whiff of what smelled like rotten eggs, and he recognized it from other hot springs he had seen. He was now in the lead and turned back to call out to Liam, "I smell the hot springs. Anybody ever get into those springs?"

"What for?" asked a frowning Liam.

"For a good bath, makes tired muscles feel mighty good!" declared Cord, remembering the hot springs enjoyed with Lone Eagle and her family of Ute.

"Ain't never seen nobody do it, but there's always some fool that'd try! Them waters are too hot!

Prob'ly boil yore skin right off!" declared Liam, frowning with all the seriousness he could muster.

Cord chuckled and kept riding toward the smell of the hot springs. He was determined to at least have a good look and maybe even try them. It had been a while since he had a good hot bath, and it was appealing. But the hot springs were disappointing for Cord—no pool, water excessively hot, and the runoff had wound its way to the Animas River below. Liam commented, "Those springs look like the earth belched up something that was disagreeable and thar she lays! Those big humps an' all those colors, the red, brown, yellow, and more, makes me think of the days when I was drinkin' too much!"

Cord shook his head, chuckling, but something further down the canyon caught his attention. He nodded to the bend of the road that twisted its way around the sloping shoulder of the hillside, and stated, "I don't like the looks of that. See there, that's six, eight turkey buzzards and they're eyeing something down there between the road and the river. Let's have a looksee," he declared, nudging Kwitcher to a canter. As they neared, it was evident it was a working mining claim, a long sluice brought water from upstream and dropped it into a long sluice box with ripples. But beyond the sluice box, three bodies were sprawled out, the end of the box had been smashed, and spades, pans, and more were scattered about. A miner's tent had been ripped and smashed, and the carcass of a mule lay beyond the tent, near a makeshift barn and corral.

Cord reined up before entering the campsite, stepped down, and motioned for Liam to stay back. "I wanna check for tracks or anything that might tell what happened here."

Liam nodded, but he also stepped down, dropped the reins of his horse and the leads of his donkeys to the ground, but quickly drove pegs into the ground to picket the animals. He did the same for Cord's horse and mule, and when finished, he stood and called out to Cord, "Find anything?"

"Yeah, looks like two riders came on 'em, shot 'em all down, stole everything of value. They got off their horses here"—pointing to the edge of the camp—"and started their doin's right away. There's empty cartridges there..." pointing near the body of one of the men. "Looks like this happened yesterday, maybe late in the day. Looks like one of 'em was cooking their supper," he said and nodded toward the remains of a cookfire with scattered pans and pots. Cord shook his head, looking about. "I think I can identify the two by their footprints and their horses." He walked to a serviceberry bush nearby, picked off some hair, looked at it before putting it in his pocket. He bent to examine the hoofprints of the horses, nodding as he touched the prints, then stood and walked toward the tent. Again, he dropped to one knee, looking at the boot prints of the perpetrators, nodding all the while.

When Liam came near, frowning, he asked, "Whatchu doin'?"

Cord pointed to the boot prints, "One of 'ems bigger, bigger prints, but deeper too. That means he's a big man, heavy, but walks with a bit of a limp. The other'n's smaller, but has a hole in the sole of his right boot. While the big foot stood back, the little one's searching the tent and such. Then the little one follows the big one as they look at the sluice, search the bodies, and then leave."

"Wal, if you ain't smarter'n you look!" declared Liam, grinning. "So, now that you know all that, are ye goin' gallivantin' about and be up to some shenanigans?"

Cord chuckled, shaking his head, "No, just tendin' to business." He pulled his vest back to reveal the marshal badge and grinned at Liam.

The Irishman's eyes grew wide, and he shook his head, "An' here I been associatin' wit' a peeler!" he grinned as he turned back to fetch the horses.

"Peeler?" asked Cord, frowning at Liam's back.

"Aye, laddie. A Peeler is Gaelic for a policeman!" He chuckled as he led the horses and mule and donkeys near.

22

CONFRONTATION

SOUTH OF THE HOT SPRINGS, THE VALLEY OF THE ANIMAS River stretched to the south and opened wide arms to accept the flow of other runoff creeks like Hermosa and Lightner Creeks and others that inter-mittently came from the high country. The green valley was bounded on the east by flat-topped mesas and hogback ridges standing guard over the flat-tops, and on the west by heavy-shouldered buttes that stretched further to the west and bounded the mineral-bearing creeks that were being explored by the gold seekers. The valley bent to the west before resuming its southerly run, offering a long and fertile valley for early settlers and creeks and promising hillsides for the many prospectors.

After burying the three bodies, Cord and Liam mounted up and headed downstream where Liam promised they would find some settlement. "Don' rightly know what kind of settlement, but wherever there's prospectors, gold, and men, there will be somebody selling grub, spirits, and other such like that appeals to the flesh, an' if'n we be lucky, there might even be some bear sign!"

Near the confluence of Hermosa Creek and the Animas River, a collection of structures had gathered, although all were temporary tent types, one had a board-covered false front that held a sign that promised, *Good Food, Good Whiskey, Good Company,* and tethered to the hitchrail out front were five horses and two mules. Another hitchrail alongside stood beside a water trough, and Liam led the way. He swung down and smacked his lips and rubbed his belly, "I been too long without wettin' my whistle! An' some good grub would do me good too!"

Cord chuckled as he stepped down, but he was more reserved as he slapped the reins of Kwitcher around the rail. He had already given the other animals a once-over, saw a big sorrel, and wanted a better look before going inside. He nodded to Liam, "You go on, if they have tables, get us one. I'll be in shortly."

Liam shook his head, but did not hesitate to do as Cord had suggested. He had an almighty thirst that motivated him, and swinging his shillelagh at his side, he eagerly stepped through the door into the darker interior of the business.

Cord casually walked around behind the horses at the hitchrail and looked closely at the tracks behind the big sorrel. As suspected, the typical barrel horseshoes showed the punched nail holes that were spaced exactly like the tracks left at the claim site with the bodies. He walked beside the big horse, stroked the animal on the neck as he passed and noticed the saddle scabbard still had a Henry rifle, 1860 model, probably from the Civil War. It was the rifle that soldiers said, "That thing can be loaded on Sunday and fired through the whole week without reloadin'!" But Cord knew the Henry had a distinctive mark left on ejected cartridge casings, like those he found at the claim. He sighed heavily, walked around the smaller paint pony, looking at the scabbarded rifle that matched the other, only appearing to have a shortened stock. Both were well-used Henrys. Cord checked the loads in his Remington pistol, slipped it back into the holster, and pushed through the doors to enter the tavern.

Liam sat at a table to the side of the entry, and at his wave, Cord walked to his side to join him, his back to the doorway and facing the bar and other tables where the patrons were gathered. He noted a mismatched couple standing at the bar, a monster of a man with broad shoulders that stood head and shoulders above both the barkeep and another man on the far side of him. He hunched over a little, his head hanging and long arms resting on the bar. Standing next to the big man was a smaller man under an out-of-place brown fedora hat. He barely cleared five feet and had sloping shoulders, and a nervous movement about him. Cord was certain these were the two men that had killed the prospectors and taken their pokes and other items.

Liam chuckled, "I got us some grub comin' and the barkeep is bringin' a bottle and glasses so we can quench our thirst right off!" He grinned, puffing out his chest with pride over his accomplishment of ordering what he wanted. His ever-present shillelagh hung on the back of his chair beside him.

When the food was brought to the table, Cord asked, "Uh, say friend. Those two at the bar, the big man and little one next to him, they been around here a spell?"

"Only seen 'em onct. Early in the week, twas. But they been payin' with gold dust e'en tho they don' look like they done any diggin'," drawled the barkeeper, standing to wipe his hands on his soiled apron. He looked at Liam, "That'll be a dollar," nodding to the plates of food and the mugs of beer.

Liam stretched out to dig in his pocket, but Cord dropped a silver dollar on the table that was quickly snatched up by the barkeep. He nodded to the men and returned to his place behind the long bar, busying himself with arranging the glasses and bottles with his back to the patrons.

Liam looked to Cord, "I be thankin' you for that —but I was gonna pay."

"Next time," replied Cord, scooting closer to the table and the food. As he pulled the tin plate closer, he lowered his voice and said, "I'm not sure how this is going to happen, but I'm not letting those two leave without at least talkin' to 'em, might even have to arrest 'em."

Liam frowned, glancing from Cord to the men at the bar and back, "If you arrest 'em, then what? Ain't no jail 'round'chere, and it's a long way to any other'n. I don' even know where there is another'n. You?"

"This is the third judicial district, and the judge is a new man, James Belford. Don't know much about him, although he has been called the *Red Headed Rooster of the Rockies,* which says a little about him, but his predecessor was Hallett and *he* traveled the circuit, in its entirety, and this third district covers the southwest portion of the territory and is the biggest district. Now, it's anyone's guess what the judges will do about courts and such. One thing for certain, if I get them to Canon City, they will have court there—after all, Canon is the district seat."

"Yeah, but gettin' 'em there—look at that big 'un, you'd hafta have a wagon just for him and it'd take you a couple weeks just to get him there!"

"Ummhmm," nodded Cord, taking a sip of the coffee that had replaced the mugs of beer. He glanced over his cup to see the two men turn away from the bar to take a table, probably to eat. The big man was even more imposing as he looked directly at Cord, frowned, and with a broad grin, laughed with a choking almost giggle. The man's eyebrows hung low over his eyes, a broad forehead with receding hairline gave him the appearance of an ape, his long arms added to the impression. But when he followed the little man, Cord frowned, recognizing the actions and movements of a man that was more child than man. He did not sit down, he dropped onto the chair that rocked back, and Cord expected it to break, but it held the huge form. The sounds that came from the two were more like a pet animal and his owner, with the big man often nodding and mumbling as the little one spoke, showing a harsh expression from under a stiff frown.

Cord, frowning, rose from his seat and approached the table of the two men. He stood near, nodded to the two men, and introduced himself, "Howdy, men, my name is Cordell Beckett, and you look a little familiar. Have you been around this area long?"

The big man nodded dumbly, drool spilling from the corner of his mouth as he muttered, "Yah, yah, yah..."

The little man said, "Don't bother us. My friend here gets mad easy and when he does, bad things happen."

"You didn't tell me your names," answered Cord, looking at the little man who appeared to be around thirty-five or forty years old, a little older than most that come to the mountains. Cord stood casually, waiting for an answer.

"I said, don't bother us," growled the little man, glaring at Cord as his hand dropped to the butt of a pistol that was tucked behind his belt at his middle.

"Well, you see, that's just it. My job *is* to bother folks, especially when they *bother* others, you know, like robbing and killing them." As Cord spoke, he had turned slightly, presenting his right shoulder toward the little man and dropped his right hand, unseen, to grab the holstered pistol. As he turned back with the pistol before him, the ratcheting sound of cocking the pistol loud in the small room. Cord scowled at the little man who was trying to grab his pistol, but because he had seated himself too close to the table, he was unsuccessful.

The firm words that came from Cord and the pistol held before him, startled the big man, and he jumped to his feet, growling and shouting, "NO! DON' DO THAT! George...ish muh frien'! He owns me!"

The statement from the man with the child's mind was surprising, and Cord stepped back, bringing the pistol to bear on the big man as well. He stated firmly, "Don't make me shoot you! I don't want to hurt you or George! Now sit down!"

The big man looked to George, back to Cord and back to George, "WhatdoIdo, wha...wha...whadoIdo Geooorge?" he held his hands out to the side and gave a pleading look to George and a sidelong glance to Cord.

Cord growled, "If he makes a move, I'll shoot you!" glaring at the little man called George.

George looked at the monster, "Tiny..." and held

out his hands, palms down—"just sit down, Tiny. He's not going to do anything."

Tiny slobbered and mumbled, looking from George to Cord, and answered, "Uh...uh...okay George...if you say so, Geeorge..." and seated himself, his big forearms laying on the table with hands flat on the table.

Cord motioned to George, "Now, slowly lift that pistol from your belt, two fingers, and drop it on the floor." As he watched George, he called out to Liam, "Hey, Liam, could you come pick up this fella's pistol for me?"

When Cord glanced to Liam, the little man, George, suddenly brought a hold-out pistol from under the flap of his jacket, cocking it as he brought it to bear, but he was suddenly rocked back on his heels when the blast of a shotgun shattered the stillness of the interior and made everyone in the place jump. Even the barkeep dropped a bottle that smashed on the hard-packed dirt floor. Cord spun back to face the little man, but he had been practically obliterated by the massive shotgun blast. Cord turned to see the source of the blast and was shocked to see Liam holding his shillelagh out before him and smoke spiraling up from the end. He realized that the harmless blackwood shillelagh was a disguised shotgun that was now held by a grinning Liam, who shrugged his shoulders as he lowered the muzzle. He said, "Well, laddie, he was gonna shoot'chu an' we couldna' have that now, could we?"

23

DILEMMA

Tiny had dropped to the floor beside George, tenderly touching him on the shoulder and repeatedly calling his name, "Geooorge...Geoorrrge...get up Geooorrge..." He choked on the words and turned a pitiful look back to Cord, "You hurt my Geoorrge... what do I do now..." he whined, cocking his big head to the side. He slowly rose, looked at Cord and at Liam, not understanding what had happened. Cord had holstered his pistol, and Liam's shillelagh hung on his forearm. "Who hurt him? You...?" he pleaded as he looked at Cord.

Tiny glared menacingly at Cord, a mixture of anger and fear flaming in his eyes. He glanced around, saw the Smith & Wesson .32 pistol laying near the outstretched hand of his friend George, and Tiny slowly reached for the weapon. But he grabbed it by the muzzle and looked at George, then to Cord,

"He wouldn't let me touch this before...but..." he stretched out his hand toward Cord, offering him the pistol grip end of the pistol, and Cord stepped closer and took the proffered weapon from the big boy/man. Tiny said, "George said that was his, uh, his...protect...protect...shun."

Cord nodded, watched as Liam came near and offered Tiny a hand up. As the boy/man came to his feet, he seemed even larger than before. Standing a full head above Cord and head and shoulders above Liam. Tiny slobbered and stuttered as he tried to talk, "What do I...do I do...now? George was muh friend an...I don' know nobody else. What...what... am I..." stammered Tiny as he started toward the door. Cord nodded to Liam to go with Tiny, and Cord turned to the others in the tavern. He looked at the barkeep, "We tracked these two from a claim at the mouth of the canyon alongside the creek. There were three dead men, the camp gear ransacked and smashed, and anything of value was gone. I'd like you to go outside to the two horses and go through the packs and such. You'll probably find some gold pokes and other things that belonged to the miners."

He turned and looked at the others at the tables that sat still, looking at Cord, and he explained, "I'm Cordell Beckett, deputy marshal for this district. I was going to arrest these two and take them to Canon City for trial, unless we could find the circuit judge before then, but..." he shrugged.

"What'chu gonna do with the dummy, Marshal?" asked one of the men at the table.

"Dunno yet, I'm going to question him, look things over. I don't think he did any of the killing, but that's yet to be determined. If I don't think he did, then I'll see what can be done to get him someone to take him in or..."

"We could take care o' that right'chere! We can muster up a miner's court, an' then hang him from one o' these big trees hereabouts!"

Some of the others laughed, nodded, and added their muttered comments. But Cord answered, "No, we'll see to that all proper and legal." He had holstered his Remington and carried the pistol of the dead man as he headed for the door. The barkeep called out, "Hey! What about the dead man?"

Cord turned, glanced from the barkeep to the dead man and to the others at the tables, "Hang him!" and walked out the door.

The barkeep followed Cord from the tavern, and Liam had seated Tiny on the edge of the boardwalk as he asked, "That big sorrel your horse?"

"Ummhmmm, that's big Red...hehehe..." Tiny chuckled, grinning and pointing to his horse. "An' that'ns George's!" pointing to the smaller paint gelding.

Liam nodded, glanced at Cord, and started going through the saddle bags and bedroll on the big horse. Cord motioned for the barkeep to do the same with the bags and bedroll on the paint. When they finished, Liam stood back and looked at Cord, "There ain't nuthin' here but a change of clothes, a wrapped slab of bacon, a bag of beans, and a skillet. The bedroll had the clothes and a couple blankets—nuthin' else!"

The barkeep had set the saddlebags on the boardwalk and looked at Cord, "Lookee here," and lifted three pouches of gold dust from the bags. "And there's some papers, looks like the claim papers, maybe some letters, dunno what all."

"Who are the letters to?" asked Cord, leaning on the hitchrail.

"Uh, looks like maybe one o' the prospector's wife. Somebody name of Mrs. Sylvia Hackworth, Louisville, Kentucky."

Cord looked to Tiny, "What was George's last name?"

"Geoorrge Jones, Jonesy, Jones!"

"Where'd those pouches come from?" asked Cord, frowning at Tiny.

The big boy/man shrugged, "George got'em from...from...those men at the...them he shot!"

"Did you shoot any men?"

"Ohhhh noooo...Geoorrge don' let me shoot..."

"But you have a rifle in the scabbard?"

"That's Geoorrge's rifle...he called it the...uh...the spare one! Hehehe..."

"Whatchu gonna do with the gold, Marshal?" asked the barkeep.

"Soon as I get to a town, I'll send it to the wife of

that man," nodding to the letters held in the barkeep's hand.

"But they owe me for drinks and food..." pleaded the barkeep.

Cord nodded to the inside of the tavern, "Go through *his* pockets, you can keep whatever *he* had."

The barkeep grinned, came to his feet, and quickly went inside before anyone else got the idea of cleaning out the dead man's pockets.

Liam looked at Cord, frowning, back to Tiny, and went to Tiny's side, seating himself beside him. "So, Tiny. What'chu gonna do now?"

"Uh...I dunno..." mumbled the big man, his head hanging.

"I've got a claim back in the mountains. If you want to come with me and help me mine the claim, I'll share with you."

Tiny lifted his head, looked at Liam, "Can I? Can I? I'd like that...yeah..."

Liam chuckled, looked at Cord, "That be alright with you? I don't think he had anything to do with the killing of those men, and he wouldn't understand anything if you took him before a judge, and they wouldn't know what to do with him. I think I can handle him, had a little experience with a friend back in the homeland 'fore I came here."

Cord leaned on the rail, looking at the pair of new friends, and slowly grinned. "I reckon that'd be the easiest thing to do, but I'd recommend you hightail it outta here before those miners in there get to drinkin' and thinkin' they need to hang somebody else."

Liam grinned, rose to his feet with the help of his shillelagh, and said to Tiny, "Let's go to the high country, my friend!" and offered his hand to help the boy/man stand.

Cord watched the two ride away, feeling good about what was done, even though a man had died. But a good man had been salvaged and might have a better life than before, and that was something to count on, especially the Irishman. Cord stepped aboard Kwitcher, grabbed the lead for the mule and with a wave to Blue, they started away from the only semblance of a settlement in this area, headed for the way back to Wagon Wheel Gap and hopefully the chance to bring another band of outlaws to justice.

———

ALBERT BROWN HAD RIDDEN with John Reynolds and his brother when they had the notorious Reynolds gang that had been captured and the others hanged. It was Brown and John Reynolds that made their escape and disappeared south into Santa Fe where they made way by gambling and a few other outlaw escapades. But they knew of the hidden stash of gold that had been left in the South Park area and were determined to retrieve the gold, but had agreed they must stay out of sight and beyond the reach of the law before returning to the area where they had been so well known.

But now, John Reynolds, who was known as Wallace, had become the confidante of the man known as Blondy, and Brown was suspecting a betrayal from John Reynolds. Thinking about it, Brown began to believe that Reynolds wanted to keep all the stash of gold to himself and not share it with Brown, and the only way that could be done would be to get rid of Brown. With a big sigh, Brown glanced over at Wallace as he and Blondy walked toward the creek by their camp, talking in low tones, their backs to the others.

They had taken a short break to rest the horses and get something to eat in an oft-used campsite on the banks of the Rio Grande upstream of the confluence with Roaring Creek. Johnny Barnes saw Brown and noticed his expression and spoke quietly, "They're kinda chummy, ain't they?"

"Yeah, I been noticin' that. Ever since we added them," nodding to three new recruits to their outlawry—"they been doin' a lot of talkin' off by themselves. I thought we were gonna be stayin' in South Park where there's more diggin's an' such, but..."

"Wal, we ain't been doin' too bad. We made out alright with them last two, an' since Wallace has decided to just make 'em pay us for *protection* and not take ever'thing, seems to be workin' alright. 'Sides, now that there's a saloon in the Gap, an' the gen'l store, what else we need?"

"I'd like more than drinkin' money. I want a good stake so's I can get outta this country!" growled Brown. "We'd had it by now if we'd stayed o'er the hill in Fairplay an' thereabouts."

"Hey, what about that wagon train that came through here? You know, the one we saw the traces from when we was comin' back from South Park, down where the Rio Grande comes from the canyon and meets up with that other'n? There had to be at least fifty or more wagons!" asked Barnes, looking at Brown.

"Wallace thot' it'd be better to wait'n see if they did some prospectin'," explained Brown.

"But them folks usually have all their savin's with 'em, and other things that are valuable. 'Sides they ain't got no law with 'em neither! An' if we go back to Fairplay, there might be somebody recognize us from before, an' Wallace kilt that fella in the saloon! And we know there's law in those places— you know, sheriffs an' such like?"

"Some. Nuthin' to worry 'bout. We can handle anything they got and there'd be 'nuff money to go 'round. Not just 'nuff for them to keep an' dole out a few dollars at a time. An' they got more'n one saloon and 'fore we left I heard they was gettin' some dancin' girls in! But what we're doin', why that's worse'n workin' a reg'lar job. I had it that good when I was ridin' for a ranch down in Santa Fe! But you know, hittin' a wagon train wit' all them farmers might not be such a bad idee! 'Sides, none of us saw them wagons, just the tracks an' such. But they was a bunch of 'em, an' it looked like they was drivin' a herd of horses too. Anyway, I'm 'bout ready to pull up stakes and head out on muh own!"

Barnes nodded to Brown, "Here they come back, we can talk more later."

24

WAGONS

CORD HAD BEEN ON THE TRAIL EAST FOR GOING ON THREE days. It was a lonesome ride, the only living things he had seen were two black bears, a small herd of elk, a pair of big bull elk, a handful of mule deer and several coyotes. He did not bother counting the jackrabbits, skunks, chipmunks or other little creatures, although he always enjoyed their many antics. He traveled the valley that lay in the shadows of the timbered foothills of the San Juan Mountains, crossing the Florida, Los Pinos, Piedra rivers and the lesser creeks called Bear, Beaver and Yellowjacket. It was a fertile land, tall gramma, bluestem, and Indian grasses waving in the breeze as he passed by and the many kinnikinnick, chokecherry and serviceberry bushes offering midday snacks.

It was a pleasant time, he was feeling much stronger. The bullet wound he suffered from the sniper bullet of the Wallace gang shooter called Dixie and ministered to by Lone Eagle, the woman shaman of the Uncompahgre Ute, was healing quite well. He often stretched his arm and shoulder, strengthening his wounded muscles, and grinned when he thought of returning the favor to the gang, knowing they would be surprised at his return.

The trail he followed probably started as a game trail, but it had been used by the natives for many years as they migrated west or east below the high mountains, and had since been used by settlers and even some freight wagons, probably carrying freight to the early settlements or soon-to-be settlements in gold country. The trail kept to the edge of the trees, following the natural contours of the lower timbered foothills, but occasionally broke into the open and offering long-distance views of the southern flats. Although he had not traveled this country before, Broken Arrow had told him of the land and the travels of his people.

Off his right shoulder on the south, marched a long hogback rim-rocked ridge with talus slopes sliding down to the valley bottom, often forcing the Piedra River to make way for the crowding rock. When he broke into the open, he was surprised by a distant sight. Sitting boldly atop a long hill were two rock formations, one looking like a great stone build-ing, the other like a proud, tall chimney. Broken Arrow had told Cord of these landmarks and also told of, "Stone buildings of the ancients. The people that came long before my people, built big buildings of stacked flat stones," he shook his head as he spoke, the wonder of the sight showing in his eyes. And it was indeed a wonder. Cord chuckled, thinking that he saw this as a wonder of God's creation, while Broken Arrow saw the smaller stones as a wonder of ancient peoples.

The hills gave way to rolling lands with fertile valleys between the lesser hills, and Cord passed several homesteads, the buildings too far from the trail for him to make a visit, but he made a mental note of the places, remembering the few home-steaders that would be the beginning of bigger settlements and more. Every water crossing showed signs of prospectors digging prospect holes or shov-eling gravel and sand from the shallows to try to find color. Some more promising places had a few prospectors actively working, and each gave a wave to the passing Cord.

It was late afternoon when the trail broke into the open with wider valleys, lower hills and fertile flatlands. A low saddle crossing between two timbered hills, both showing tall ponderosa and scattered juniper trees, beckoned Cord onward. But the sight of a trio of riders before him painted a frown on Cord's face, until he recognized his long-time friend, Broken Arrow, the leader of the Wolf-pack Warriors of the Uncompahgre Ute people. He came from the shadows of the ponderosa, his right hand lifted, open palm, and a grin on his usually very stoic face as the two friends neared one another.

"Well, Broken Arrow, I did not expect to see you around these parts!" The two came close, extending their hands and clasping forearms in the typical greeting of the native people.

"I had seen you before and knew you would come this way. We are making camp, will you camp with us?"

"Of course, glad for the company. I've even got some fresh meat to share. Got me a young buck back along the trail a ways, planned on havin' some good meat for supper."

"It is good."

———

AFTER THEIR MEAL, Cord sat with Broken Arrow and the stoic Ute warrior looked at Cord, "There are many wagons camped near the hot springs. We could not go to the springs as we planned. Too many White men!" grumbled Broken Arrow.

"How many wagons?" asked Cord.

Broken Arrow flashed all fingers of both hands three times, "This many! They do not know this is the land of the Uncompahgre? They must leave!" he declared, hitting his fist on his knee.

"I will talk to them. See what they're up to, what they're planning. Then I'll explain to them this is your land and they must leave. But there's only so much I can do."

"They have buffalo men with them, what you call so'jers."

"Buffalo men?" asked Cord, frowning.

"They are the color of the buffalo, have hair like the big bull buffalo," declared Broken Arrow, touching his skin and his hair as he spoke.

Cord slowly grinned as he realized what Broken Arrow meant. He knew that there were many coloreds that had joined the Union army and were still serving long after the Civil War ended and had been stationed in Fort Lyon and Fort Garland. This was probably the first time these native people had encountered the colored cavalry, but Cord wondered why the cavalry would be traveling with the wagons of settlers.

———

LONG SHADOWS STRETCHED behind Cord as he rode from the camp and his friends. They had returned to the mountains on their hunt, but Cord was now riding to meet the members of the wagons that were camped near the hot springs. The trail bent around a low butte and pointed northward across the rolling hills that were occasionally dotted by homesteader cabins, but the juniper, piñon, and twisted cedar offered ample cover. Cord pushed on, and after cresting a couple lower hills, he reined up, surprised to see the encampment of so many wagons. Their pale bonnets looking like sails in the morning sun that was just cresting the mountains beyond. While the tall granite peaks of the San Juans scratched at the blue of the morning sky, the dark timbered foothills blanketed the edges of the valley that Cord estimated to be about three by five miles of rolling hills and fertile plains. He could see why settlers would be impressed with the land, a land that whispered promises of those looking for a home and perhaps more.

He nudged Kwitcher closer, and as he neared the encampment, he was spotted by a woman throwing out a bucket of wash water. She was startled by this stranger in the long duster and atop the grulla stallion, and turned to holler at her man, who came running, rifle in hand. As Cord came near, the man shouted, "Stop right there! State yore bizness or move along!" The shouting had caught the attention of others, and several people gathered at the edge of the two wagons where the man and woman stood, some muttering questions, others shading their eyes to look at the visitor.

"Just comin' to talk to you folks—who's in charge?" asked Cord, pushing his high-crowned hat back on his head and leaning forward on the pommel of his saddle.

"That'd be Whitcomb, Riley Whitcomb, he's our wagon master!" answered the rifleman with a shout. But others behind him also called out, "Or Colonel

Hatch of the Ninth!" As they spoke, Cord saw a few uniformed soldiers, all colored, at the edge of the crowd.

"Be glad to talk to 'em both, if you'll bring 'em out!" answered Cord, then asked, "Alright if I step down?"

"Go 'head, but don't try nuthin'!" ordered the rifleman.

Cord chuckled at the thought of one man going against the people of about thirty wagons accompanied by a company of cavalry, but stepped down and stood beside Kwitcher's head, reins held loosely at his side and Blue belly down, tongue lolling, beside him. He did not have to wait but a moment or two when three men, one in uniform, another with the typical attire of a settler topped off with a wide-brimmed black flat-topped hat, and the third with a lop-sided sombrero, came to the fore. The colonel stepped closer, motioning to Cord, "Come on in, friend, we can talk over some coffee. How's that sound?"

"Sounds good, I could use some good coffee 'bout now," answered Cord, as he led Kwitcher and the mule with Blue at his side. He nodded to the colonel, "Let me take care of my animals first, and I'll be right along!" With a nod from the colonel, Cord led Kwitcher to the rope corral where some of the riding stock of the people was kept and loosed the rope, moved Kwitcher inside, loosened the cinch, and tossed the reins over his neck, letting him sniff out the others. He did the same with the mule and motioned Blue to follow at his heel. He left the corral and followed the colonel into the separate encampment that was beyond the wagons. Both the wagon masters and the colonel took a seat at a table that was under the outstretched canvas flap of the colonel's tent, and the colonel motioned for Cord to be seated. Before being seated, Cord extended his hand to the first of the wagon masters and introduced himself, "I'm Cordell Beckett and you are?"

The man stood, extending his hand and answered, "I'm Riley Whitcomb, I'm leading the wagons that came from Fort Garland."

Cord shook his hand and nodded, then turned to the second man, a question on his face as he extended his hand. The man stood, "I'm John Martinez, of Santa Fe. Our wagons came from Santa Fe, and we're bound for the mountains, maybe find some land and some gold, much like this," waving his hand around to indicate the land in the valley to the west of them. He shook Cord's hand and took a seat.

As Cord seated himself, he purposely pulled the flap of his leather vest back to reveal the marshal badge, but did not otherwise bring any attention to it or himself.

"Now, what prompts this visit? Just passing through or..." the colonel shrugged, glancing from the badge to the wagon masters and back to Cord.

Cord grinned, sat back when an orderly started

pouring cups full of fresh hot coffee. As the orderly left, Cord leaned forward, looking directly at the colonel, "First, let me ask you, why the soldiers?"

"Why, to protect the settlers, why else?"

"Do you know this is the land of the Ute people, designated as such by the 1868 treaty with Kit Carson and others?"

"Yes, I know that. But these people were insistent on coming through, and those traveling with Mr. Martinez met us here, strictly coincidental."

Cord looked at Martinez, "Did you know this is native land protected by the treaty?"

"No, I did not. I understood this was open for settlement under the Homestead Act. The authorities in Santa Fe assured me this was open land."

Cord dropped his eyes as he slowly shook his head, then looking up, explained, "I just had a visit from Broken Arrow, the leader of the Warriors of the Wolf of the Uncompahgre Ute, and he told me about your wagons being here, on what he called, well, sacred land or what we would consider to be Holy Land to the natives. Chief Ouray had asked me to be his interpreter and assist him in any negotiations regarding treaties to which I agreed. Now, what are your plans?" asked Cord, looking from one to the other of the men.

"Well, surely the natives would not do anything that would make matters worse. You know, they would not attack such a large group as this, would they?" asked the colonel.

Cord grinned, "How many men do you have here, Colonel? Not just soldiers, but other fighting men?"

"Well, we have about a half-company of men, about fifty, and the men of the wagons..." he looked to the wagon masters for their input.

Whitcomb answered, "We have maybe twenty-five men that could fight if need be," then turned to Martinez, "And we have about the same," he nodded.

"So, maybe you could put together about a hundred fighting men, with women and children all about the wagons. Ouray could bring twice that many, all proven warriors and well-armed, and if need be, he could call on the Weeminuche and Tabe-guache, for another two hundred, and other bands of the greater Ute people for many more." He paused, looking from one to the other of the men.

"This land has been the homeland of the Ute people for generations. Every significant place, like the hot springs here, or the Treasure Falls back in the hills, or the Chimney Rock, are places that have special meaning for the people. Like Chimney Rock, where the ancients, a people sometimes known as the Pueblo or cliff dwellers, built a special place to worship, what you might call a church or cathedral, atop that mountain. The ruins are still there today. And there are memories, stories, and more about all this land. And the whites that come, take it away from them, and dig it up, destroy the land, all on the slim possibility they might find gold." He looked around the table at the men, then added, "Kit Carson helped negotiate the last treaty that called for all the land from the crest of the mountains west, from the White and Yampa Rivers in the north, and the New Mexico border in the south, to be the land of the Ute people forever. And that, my friends, includes this land where you now sit." Cord sat back, sighed heavily, and looked at the three men before him.

25

FACE-OFF

"So...that badge? That mean you're a lawman around these parts?" asked Whitcomb, obviously upset with the man that sat before him and telling him they could not do what they had traveled so far to build new lives.

Cord leaned back, pulled the vest aside, "That says I'm a deputy marshal for this third district of Colorado Territory."

"And what does that mean as far as us continuing our journey?"

"Nothing, as long as you keep going."

Martinez looked at Cord, scowling, "We have come from Santa Fe on the promise of new land. Our people have left behind families, homes, and more—just to try to make a new home."

Whitcomb added, "And if you had been with us gettin' over those mountains," pointing to the eastern foothills of the San Juans—"you might be thinkin' different about these people. They, too, left homes, families, and more, and risked their lives in the doin' of it!"

Cord shook his head, lifted his eyes and answered, "And the people of the Ute who have made this their home for the last, oh, I don't know, maybe four, five hundred years, are willing to fight for their homes. Just like you and your people would do if the natives were attacking their homes."

The three men looked at one another, grumbling as they scowled at Cord until Colonel Hatch spoke up, "Well, gentlemen, it appears we are at an impasse. I suggest we think about what the possible options might be while we have a meal and talk with the others. After all, it's not just our decision. We, the men of the Ninth, have been tasked to keep you all safe, but that does not mean starting an Indian war! So...talk to your people and then we'll talk again." He nodded from one to the other and stood, motioning to Cord to follow him away from the table.

As they moved away, the colonel glanced back at the leaders of the wagons and lowered his voice as he spoke, "Marshal, I would appreciate it if you would stay around a day or so, at least until we get these people back on the move and away from here. I'm not sure what they'll do, but at least getting them away from the sacred lands of the people would be a help. I cannot force them to do anything, and each man is responsible for his own doings. I just hope they won't be too much trouble."

"I can stay a day or so, and it might help if I am here just in case the Ute show up again, and I kinda expect they will," replied Cord.

"You're welcome to make your camp near ours," he pointed to the edge of the trees where the command tent sat and the other shelters of the men were gathered. Cord nodded and walked away to fetch his gear and bedroll.

"WE CAN'T BE TOO FAR behind them, prob'ly catch up to 'em sometime tomorrow," suggested Blondy, glancing sideways at John Reynolds.

"Yeah, but then what? We ain't even sure they got anything worth goin' after," grumbled Reynolds, better known among this bunch as Wallace. "Why'd we ever listen to them?" nodding to the five men following.

"Cuz we din't have nothin' better! The gold diggers 'round the Gap were tapped out and runnin' out, an' weren't nothin' better nowheres else! So... this seemed like as good an idea as any. 'Sides, we'll be gettin' into new country an' from what I hear, that side of these here mountains shows more promise. I even heard some o' them diggers talkin' 'bout it o'er to Fairplay an' such."

"Wal, mebbe," grumbled Wallace, scowling at

Blondy and giving a glance to the followers. Brown, Barnes, and the three newbies trailed behind them, but together, Wallace had a little more confidence in their numbers. After losing four of his men to the upstart marshal that Dixie finally killed, he believed this bunch was as good as any he had ever mustered. After their trek back into South Park and failing to get to the buried loot left behind by his brother and the rest of the Reynolds gang, he needed more money if he was going to make another try for the loot, especially if he could do it alone, or at least with just one or two of the others.

Blondy reined up and pointed, "Hey! Lookee thar'!" he was motioning to the bottom of the draw where the Wolf Creek had cut away a rocky bank and a pair of prospectors were anxiously digging in the gravel face, excited about what they were finding and oblivious to any company.

With the others stopped in the trail behind them, Blondy and Wallace kept themselves hidden in the trees as they watched the excited prospectors. Blondy said, "They're excited about sumpin'!"

"Yeah, but they ain't dug enough to get much!" complained Wallace.

"Don't take much to get me excited. Couple o' good nuggets will do it!"

Wallace swung to the ground, nodded to the others, "We're gonna check 'em out. The rest of you wait here!"

Blondy joined Wallace as they moved from the

thicker trees and found a game trail that would take them to the bottom of the steep-sided draw and get them closer to the prospectors. As they neared, they heard one of the diggers shout, "Look at this! Bigger'n anything we found so far!"

The other one grunted and kept digging. They were shoveling the loose gravel into a pile beside the creek bed, probably to pan out with the water later. Now they were looking for a vein or heavier lode gold, the kind that produced nuggets. Their excitement masked the approach of the two outlaws and when Blondy shouted, "Git'chur hands up! Drop them shovels!" the two men jumped back, eyes wide, mouths open, as they lifted their hands. The bigger of the two whiskery faced men wet himself as he started to plead, "No mister—don' shoot! I don' wanna die!"

Blondy and Wallace squinted and turned their faces away slightly as they saw what the man had done. But that was what the miner wanted—he grabbed up a nearby shotgun and let go with both barrels, the double-ought buckshot lifting Blondy off his feet and dropping his bloodied carcass on the rocks just above the water and within seconds, his blood was coloring the water of Wolf Creek.

The blast of the miner left his shotgun empty, but Wallace returned the favor as he emptied his pistol in the two men, painting their fronts with blood, and one bullet taking the top off one of the men's heads as he stumbled backwards over his own shovel.

Wallace stood with his pistol smoking as he shook his head and muttering expletives. He looked at the remains of Blondy and called out, "Hey Brown! C'mon down here, give me a hand!"

Brown looked at the others, all of whom had dismounted and were sitting in the shade of some towering ponderosa, and stood to his feet, tossed the reins of his mount to Barnes and started from the trees to see what all the shooting was about. When he approached Wallace, who was sitting on an outthrust rock, his elbows on his knees, Wallace said, "See if they got anything in their pockets, look around see if you can find a pouch or anything. The way they was talkin' they musta found a nugget or two, so look for that. I'm goin' back up there, and have the rest of 'em start makin' camp."

"How 'bout sendin' Barnes down here to help me look an' mebbe cover up these bodies so they won't start stinkin' and ruin our camp cookin'?"

"Yeah, yeah..." answered Wallace, rising from the rock and starting up the narrow trail.

When Barnes joined Brown, he was already going through the pockets of the first miner and Brown nodded to the other one, "You look o'er that'n, then we'll go through their diggin's."

"They got a camp nearby anywhere?" asked Barnes as he bent over the dead miner.

"Dunno, ain't had time to look." He glanced at Barnes and saw the man had his back to him which prompted Brown to grin as he pocketed a thumb-sized nugget. What Brown did not see was Barnes doing the same thing with a slightly larger nugget from the other miner's pocket.

"Findin' anything?" asked Brown, "you know, a pouch or anything?"

"Nunhuhn..." mumbled Barnes, standing and turning to face Brown. "You?"

"Nuthin' I wanna share," answered a grinning Brown, with a glance up the trail as he patted his pocket.

Barnes chuckled, patted his own pocket, "Let's see if we can find a camp nearby."

All they found was a nearby flat with two tethered burros, some stacked packs with minimal rations, some tools and pans, and a bag of raggedy clothes. Barnes looked to Brown and said, "We heard them two hollerin' 'bout findin' a nugget so we better have sumpin' to show or Wallace'l start shootin' agin."

"Yeah, mebbe we better give him what we got, or...mebbe just one. We can share the other'n."

When they returned, they showed long faces but handed over the bigger of the two nuggets, Brown keeping his hidden in his trousers pocket. He declared, "That's all they had boss, they din't even make camp. They had a couple burros back yonder, nuthin' worthwhile cep'n some tools and pans, but no pouches or nuthin'."

Wallace looked at the nugget, grinning, stuffed it in his pocket, and looked back at the two with a nod.

"Then let's have some supper, get some sleep, an' we'll get after them wagons come mornin', less'n we find us some more diggers!" he cackled, as he sat on the moss-covered log in the shade of a wide spreading juniper.

26

COUNCIL

THE WAGONS FROM FORT GARLAND AND LED BY RILEY Whitcomb, had been on the trail for over a month and had hard going getting over the mountains on the trail that had never been traveled by wagons, except a few smaller freighters or carts used by the earlier settlers and prospectors. And some of the families had been on the trail for several months, coming from as far away as Missouri, Illinois, Arkansas, and Kansas, all in hope of a new homestead of at least 160 acres of virgin land. After the strenuous crossing of the lower San Juan Mountains, they needed a rest and time to repair their wagons and more. The hot springs were especially appealing to tired muscles and bodies, and a refreshing for those that had not enjoyed a hot bath for months.

The trail brought them into the valley by following the upper reaches of the San Juan River and after a couple dog-leg bends to the south, the river offered an easy crossing to the north shore just after the river split a long stretch of high timber-covered buttes, where they made their camp. The larger butte on the south side rose a good five hundred feet under its hoary head of tall dark green ponderosa and fir trees, and the soldiers had made their camp on the south shore, nearer the cover of the tall timber of the butte and away from the wagons.

But that butte had a basin near the crest that offered a favored campsite for the people of the Tabeguache or Uncompahgre Ute. The temporary camp sheltered the many warriors that had been assembled by Broken Arrow at the behest of Chief Ouray, to protect the sacred waters of the hot springs they called *Pagwöösa*. There had been others of the White men that had defiled the springs and they were determined to protect the sacred waters from these unwanted invaders of their lands.

Cord had spotted a thin line of smoke that rose from the thick woods just before dusk and he grinned, knowing that would probably be where Broken Arrow and his warriors would be and he also knew that the smoke had been for him and him alone for it was not something his people would do —to allow a cookfire to give away their location, unless they wanted.

When Cord came from his blankets just before first light, he looked around the camp and with rifle in hand, binoculars hanging around his neck, and his

Bible in the other hand, he started his climb up the big butte. The chill of the mountain air before sunrise crawled down Cord's neck, making him give an involuntary shiver as he chuckled to himself, thinking about the times he complained because of the heat of midday sun. The sweet smell of pines filled his lungs as he trudged up the steep game trail, and the faint light of morning gave just enough for Cord to keep from stepping on the brittle pine cones that would give away his presence, while the long needles of the ponderosa offered a blanket of silence to each footfall. But he was brought up short by the clear voice of Lone Eagle, the woman shaman of the people.

"It is good to see you my friend," she spoke, only loud enough for Cord to hear and recognize the voice of the woman that had occupied his thoughts for the last year and more.

"And it is good to see you, Lone Eagle."

"I knew you would be coming. I want to speak with you before you meet with my brother, Broken Arrow."

Cord nodded, motioned to a slight clearing on a small shoulder of the hill that offered a view of the valley below and a massive, partially buried boulder that invited them to seat themselves. Lone Eagle also carried a rifle and placed it beside her, moving to the edge so Cord could be seated near. He lay his Bible between them, his rifle to his left, and sat close to the beautiful woman who seemed to glow in the morning light as the sun began to tell of its rising by painting the sky in pale shades of pink and orange behind the butte.

He smiled and asked, "Broken Arrow planning something, is he?"

Lone Eagle nodded, her face showing no emotion as she dropped her eyes, "He is angry with the people of the wagons. Others have come through and passed on, but these...they spoil the sacred waters with their waste, their filth, and more."

Cord frowned, "I did not know this. The leaders of the wagons said the people have done nothing but bathe in the river and wash clothes on that side, away from the hot springs water. Yes, the waters do flow into the river there, but on the far side, it is just warm and more suitable for what they do."

"But they do come to this side of the river, the soldiers do also. Several have bathed in the spring waters in the smaller and lower pools. That is not bad, and I understand, but when they throw their waste and filth and more...that is our sacred waters and that is what angers Broken Arrow. I believe he will try to drive all these people away."

"Drive them away? You mean fight them?"

"If they choose to do so, he will fight. All the Warriors of the Wolf are here, and more. We have many young warriors, unproven, that seek to gain their warrior honors."

Cord knew the only way young men could gain those honors was by killing the enemy and in times of peace, to kill many game animals to feed the people, but those that kill an enemy need only kill one. Cord dropped his eyes, slowly shaking his head and looked up at Lone Eagle, "I was afraid of that. There are those down there that want to stay here and build homes and make this their land."

"But the treaty..." began Lone Eagle, frowning as she looked at Cord.

"I know, and I've told them about that, but they have traveled many days, months even, and they are tired, and this *is* beautiful country! I believe some are thinking it might be worth fighting for, and they have many fighting men as well as the soldiers that Broken Arrow calls Buffalo Soldiers."

"What can be done to stop it? I mean, to stop the wagon people from defiling the hot springs?"

"What can be done to stop the fighting? There are many of the wagon people that are afraid of anyone that even *speaks* of the Ute people, and if Broken Arrow and the warriors show themselves, they might just start shooting!"

Lone Eagle lowered her eyes, spoke softly, "Is that the way you feel?"

"No! Of course not. You know me better than that! I have nothing but respect and love for you and your people. I understand what you have been through and what you have overcome. But..." he shrugged, nodded toward the valley and the many wagons, "those people have been through a lot themselves.

Most of the men were in the recent war and lost their homes. Now they've come out here to try to make a new home for their families, and it's hard for them to understand why they cannot. They look around and see so much, the fertile valleys, the mountains, and they've never seen land like this, and they want to live here. You can understand that, can't you?"

"Yes. But your people made a treaty that said this land," she waved her hand to encompass the entire valley and the mountains around, "was to be our land forever. And now, these people come to take it from us. That is not right! We cannot trust the leaders of your people that say one thing and do not keep their word. Among my people, when you give your word, it must be kept—be sacred to you, and never broken!"

"And with many of us, that is true. But there are those that do not live that way. Just like some among your people that do not follow the law of your people and do not do as the leaders say, or what they have agreed."

Lone Eagle leaned against Cord, her head against his shoulder, and her eyes down. Quietly, she added, "We must talk to our people. Try to prevent this." She knew she did not have to explain *this* to Cord, because the times they spent together, they began to understand one another completely, and she knew he thought as she did about keeping the peace between their peoples.

————

WHEN CORD WALKED BACK into the camp of the
soldiers, they were already busy at their campfires,
preparing their morning meals with as many as five
or six around each fire. He walked to the comman-
dant's tent and announced himself, "Colonel? It's
Cordell Beckett. Do you have a couple minutes? We
need to talk."

The answer came from within, "Be right out
Beckett. Have a seat. My orderly will get you some
coffee."

Cord did as bidden and appreciated the orderly
pouring him a cup of fresh steaming coffee. He sat
back in the canvas chair, crossed his legs, and looked
around. The encampment of the soldiers was on the
south bank of the San Juan River while the wagons
were circled up on the north side, but they were still
within shouting distance. He saw a few women
already down at water's edge, either fetching water
or rinsing out some laundry. Cookfires were going
and fine pillars of smoke curled towards the sky that
had already shed the colors of the sunrise. It was a
serene setting, but like many peaceful appearing
scenes, things could change in a moment.

"Mornin' Beckett! What brings you out so early?"
greeted the colonel as he finished buttoning his
uniform blouse and nodded to the orderly to pour his
coffee. He seated himself and looked at Cord, waiting
for an answer.

"Well, Colonel. I've been talking to the leader of the Ute people, and they're not too happy with all these folks in their land and especially with those that have defiled the sacred springs."

The colonel frowned, reached for his coffee, "I don't understand. What do you mean, *defiled?*"

"To them, these waters are sacred and are to be respected. Even the Diné, or the Navajo people see them as sacred. As a matter of fact, Navajo legend says the springs are the way their people came into this world. But..." he paused, sipped his coffee. "The Ute have seen these people throw trash into the springs, use the springs to wash their dirty laundry, and even saw one man relieve himself in the springs. Right now, they are waiting word of your leaving willingly or if they should *make* you leave!"

"Now hold on there! Ain't nobody, especially a bunch of savages, gonna *make* us do anything!" he growled, scowling at Cord.

Cord chuckled, grinned, and said, "This *is* their land and you and your men, and these people, are breaking the treaty and the law by being here. They are in the right, and if they decide to come against you in force..." he shrugged, sat back, and looked at the colonel.

"Force? They couldn't get enough men together to go against us in a month!" growled the colonel, scowling.

"Colonel. Right now, you are in the sights of one of their best shooters and if you do something he doesn't like, he will shoot! And not only that, there's probably about fifty warriors right up there in those trees that could do the same for most of your men. I was just with Broken Arrow and Lone Eagle, the leaders of the fiercest fighting force among the entire Ute nation, and they are waiting for something to happen. He has a bunch of young warriors that are quite anxious to earn their honors as a warrior by killing an enemy!"

The colonel twisted around in his chair to look at the trees, but he saw nothing. He turned back to look at Cord and said, "I don't appreciate what you're doing, marshal or not. There's no one there!" he growled.

Cord chuckled, stood, cupped his hands and spoke, "Broken Arrow! Come join us to talk!"

The colonel stood and turned to see the leader of the Wolf Pack step from the shadows and walk closer. The colonel looked from Broken Arrow to Cord and back, stammering, "But...but...but..."

Cord chuckled but said nothing, just waited for Broken Eagle to come closer. The impressive leader loosely carried a Henry rifle in one hand, wore fringed buckskin leggings, a horn-pipe beaded breastplate, wide beaded armbands, a bear claw necklace, and three feathers standing tall from a fur headpiece. The stoic expression on his face showed no compromise, and the piercing eyes made the colonel wilt as he started to seat himself but was stopped when Cord said softly, "Please stay standing. If you are seated, that is an insult."

The colonel extended his hand, "I'm Colonel Hatch of the Ninth Cavalry. You are Broken Arrow?"

"I am Broken Arrow of the Uncompahgre Ute people. We are led by Chief Ouray. I am the leader of the Warriors of the Wolf," explained Broken Arrow as he accepted the hand of the colonel and shook it briefly. He nodded to Cord as Cord motioned for him to be seated.

27

CONFLICT

THE COLONEL MOTIONED TO THE ORDERLY TO BRING CUPS and coffee and sat down opposite Broken Arrow. Cord sat between the men and leaned forward on the table, looking from one to the other. When the orderly finished pouring the coffee, Cord began with, "Now, Broken Arrow, tell the colonel here what you want to see happen here."

Broken Arrow also leaned forward, but as he started to speak, gunfire broke out at the river's edge, between the camps of the soldiers and the wagons. Shouting and screams punctuated what had been the stillness of the morning, and war cries and shouts from warriors added to the cacophony. Cord, the colonel, and Broken Arrow all came to their feet, looking toward the ruckus, and Cord and Broken Arrow started toward the river at a run, side by side. The colonel had turned to the orderly and looked to the tents to see several of the uniformed men hustling toward the sounds of fighting.

Broken Arrow had outdistanced the others and rallied his men, forcing them to retreat to the trees. Cord had splashed across the shallows to go to those that were on the north bank, shooting at the retreating natives, and he saw several of the soldiers dropping behind a slight swell to take cover and fire toward the natives. His first glance showed the body of one warrior lying belly down in the dirt, another limping away and being helped by Broken Arrow. But before him, sprawled on the ground between the river's edge and the wagons was the body of one of the settlers, face up, sightless eyes staring at the rising sun, and a distraught woman screaming and weeping as she looked at what must be her man.

Cord ran to the men gathered at the break in the wagons, taking cover behind barrels, chairs, and other miscellaneous gear. He stood before them, hands raised to quiet the shouting and threats. One man hollered, "Git outta the way less'n you want us to shoot you too! You ain't nuthin' but one o' them injun lovers nohow!"

Cord gritted his teeth against his rising anger and shouted, "I'm Deputy Marshal Cordell Beckett, and the next man that shoots will be arrested!"

The men looked around, anger showing, mumbling, but Cord continued, "Your wagon master was supposed to talk to you last night, but it apparently didn't do any good! Now—all of you are breaking the law! This is Ute territory—land guaranteed to them by the treaty of 1868! This is not land that is open for homesteads! The Ute people are within their rights to try to drive you off their lands —just like you would be within your rights if someone came onto your property!"

"You cain't arrest us all! You're only one man against all of us, an' we came all this way to stake a homestead and start a new life! I ain't affeered o' them injuns!" The talker looked around at the other men, lifted his rifle high, "What say, men? Shall we shoot our way through this bunch o' redskins?"

Cord had slipped his pistol from the holster, and as the man waved the rifle overhead, Cord quickly shot, his bullet shattering the forestock of the rifle, making the man drop it like it was molten steel. He spun around to look at Cord, anger flaring in his eyes that was quickly replaced by fear when he found himself staring down the muzzle of Cord's Remington .44 pistol. Cord kept his eyes on the man and shouted to the others, "Who's next? But next time I won't be shooting at the rifle—it'll be right between your eyes! In case you haven't figgered it out —I'm not a patient man!"

The crowd mumbled and stirred about, looking at one another, most staring at Cord, some looking at the soldiers across the river who now stood in a skirmish line, the colonel at their side. The colonel stepped forward, called out with a loud voice, "Men!

My assignment was to keep you safe! But I was also cautioned to keep you away from the natives and to do whatever is necessary to prevent any conflict! Now, you wanna go against the natives—you'll have to come through us!"

The wagonmaster, Riley Whitcomb, stepped to the front of the crowd, waved and motioned toward the timber, then hollered to the colonel, "Looks like they done high tailed it anyway, colonel!"

Cord waved for the colonel to come across the shallows, then turned back to the others, "Don't count on it. They prefer to fight from horseback and they have their horses up top there where they've been camped. They also have other warriors waiting to get in on the fighting. I would not be surprised if they are not right now, circling around to come at you from two or three different sides. So, what caused this to start?" he asked, motioning to the river's edge.

A matronly woman, grey-haired, and quite buxom, stepped forward, "That'n yonder," pointing to the dead man—"allus was a little trigger-happy. Been braggin' 'bout how he was gonna get him a injun, show 'em who was gonna rule the roost 'round 'chere. He thought his girlfriend, that'n there," she pointed to the weeping woman who Cord noted was not very old, but probably nearing marrying age, "needed to be impressed at what kinda man he was, so he stepped out there and fired at the first feather he seen. So, now she knows exactly what kinda man he was, a dumb one!" she growled, shaking her head.

"What's his name?"

"Aloysius Abernathy," answered the big woman, then in a lower voice added, "muh youngest." She turned her back on Cord, motioned to the others and watched as her man and two older sons pushed through the crowd to fetch the body. The woman started back to her wagon, the people stepping aside for her as she shook her head and wiped her tears.

As the colonel came from the shallows, wet boots and all, he stepped closer to Cord, asked, "Now what?"

Cord saw the two wagon masters come close as well, and he offered, "I think if you get these folks packed up and on the move, I might be able to prevent any more bloodshed. I can't guarantee it, but that's all they wanted, and since that young man fired the first shot, it might satisfy 'em." He sighed heavily and looked around, frowning as he noticed the body of the Ute warrior was gone. He moved side to side, looking at the tree line and as far down the line as possible. "They've already come for the body, but I don't see any movement anywhere, and that could mean they are getting ready to make an all-out assault. I suggest you get these folks moving, Colonel!"

The colonel looked at the two leaders of the wagons, "You heard the man. Unless you think you can handle a couple hundred mad warriors, I suggest you get the people moving."

"That ain't gonna be easy, Colonel," answered Whitcomb. "I already heard some talkin' about givin' that boy a decent burial and others grumbling about havin' to leave 'fore they were ready." He looked from the colonel to Cord as he spoke.

The colonel responded, "If you stay any longer, you might have to see about giving a decent burial to a bunch of others. You want that?"

"Uh, no, reckon not," replied Whitcomb, looking from the colonel to Martinez, the other wagon master. "What do you think, John?"

"Well, I don't have any trigger-happy youngsters among my people, but I do have many hot-blooded Mexicans that don't like to run from a fight. But...I'll see what I can do!" he answered.

The colonel looked at Cord, "And I'll get my men to packin' up and saddled up as well. Maybe if they see that, they'll know we're on our way."

"Hopefully. In the meantime, I'm also gonna get my horse saddled, but I'll be ridin' up into those trees to see if I can find 'em and talk 'em down," offered Cord, as he turned away and went to the shallows to cross over to the rope corral where Kwitcher and the mule were penned with the other horses. He whistled for Kwitcher, grinned as the grulla stallion came from the crowd, and Cord lifted the rope barrier and led his big horse from the herd. Kwitcher was closely followed by the mule, and Cord set about saddling Kwitcher and rigging the pack saddle and packs for the mule. He made short work of the task and swung aboard, waved at the watching colonel, and dug heels to the stallion to head into the trees, closely followed by his faithful dog, Blue.

As he crested the shoulder that overlooked the basin where they had camped, all that remained were the fire circles, and even those had been obliterated by the passing of horses. From the sign, he could tell they had split up into two groups, and as he suspected, one headed over the timbered rise on the east, and he knew that would probably take them further upstream, where they would cross over and come at the wagons through the gap in the buttes that led to the larger flats in the north. The second and larger bunch crossed to the south and that would take them downstream of the San Juan River, allowing them to cross through the cut between the buttes and across the river, well out of sight of the wagons. That would also allow them to come at the wagons from the southwest. He turned to look through the thin trees to see the wagons below, and from his promontory, he saw little or no activity, certainly not enough to show they were readying to leave. He nudged Kwitcher closer to the tree line, where he could look below at the army encampment, and they were hustling about as the colonel promised. It was evident they were breaking camp, putting their shelters and tents and gear on the pack mules, and the horses had been saddled and stood in a picket line, awaiting the soldiers. Cord mumbled to himself, "Well, Colonel Hatch, I'm hopin' you can stop this, otherwise that river's gonna run red and it won't all be Ute blood!"

He kicked Kwitcher to a canter and followed the larger group, believing Broken Arrow would be leading this group. They had crossed over a slight rise, dropping to the south side and narrowing down to file through the thicker aspen that grew close in the low swale. He could tell by the tracks they had walked their mounts down the hillside, but once they broke into the open, they picked up the pace to a slow canter, raising little dust and covering the ground quickly. The trail was easy going, a small meandering creek in the bottom of the valley trickled along, laughing its way over the ripples to carry fresh mountain spring water to join the waters of the San Juan.

As the trail rounded the point of the butte, it dropped below a slight shoulder with an overhang of rimrock, just enough to mask their crossing as the warriors lay low on the backs of their mounts. Cord spotted them as they were crossing and dug heels to Kwitcher to try to catch up with the bunch. The leaders led them from the waters into a cut between two low-rising buttes that kept them from the sight of the wagons. Cord whistled his shrill whistle that mimicked the call of the meadowlark, and he caught the attention of the lagging warriors. They instantly turned and raised their rifles, but quick recognition on the part of one or two kept them from firing on the man who was their friend. They motioned him on, and he soon came to the side of Broken Arrow who halted the others.

28

FIRE

"BROKEN ARROW—WE'VE GOT TO STOP THIS! THERE'S TOO much at stake! More of your warriors will die and many settlers will die, and what will that accomplish?" pleaded Cord, as he leaned stiff-armed forward on the pommel of his saddle. "You don't want this, do you?"

"This is our land! They have made themselves our enemy when they killed our warriors!" growled a very angry Broken Arrow. "We did as you asked, we talked, but that did nothing! Now..." he motioned to his men to follow.

Cord pleaded again, "I thought you wanted peace! But I can see I was wrong!" He shook his head, reined Kwitcher away, grumbling to himself, "Maybe I can talk some sense into the settlers!" and leaned forward on the neck of Kwitcher who responded with a long, stepping lunge forward, head outstretched as he took to the urging of his rider and broke into an all-out run, kicking clods of earth high in the air behind him. Cord lay low on the neck of his big grulla, and the mule was stretching out alongside. Blue was keeping pace with his friends and refused to be left behind.

As Cord neared the wagons, he waved and shouted, "It's Marshal Beckett! Take cover! You're about to be attacked!" He skidded the big grulla to a stop as he swung to the ground, his right boot hitting dirt just as the horse slid to a stop, his rear and tail dragging the ground. The mule veered off and stumbled to a stop before reaching the length of his lead that brought his head around to face the horse.

Cord leaped the tongue of the closest wagon and confronted the settlers, "The Ute are gathering out yonder, and they're getting ready to attack! You best get your wagons closer together, take cover, and get ready to defend yourselves!"

One blustery man who held a rifle across his chest, glared at Cord from under a single line of eyebrows and growled, "Thot you said they was peaceable!"

"That was before you killed two of their men! Now they're ready to paint this valley with your blood!"

"Can't you stop them?" pleaded a woman who huddled two small children before her.

"That time is past! You folks were asked to leave and didn't and now they..." pointing back toward the low hills to the west—"think they have to convince you to leave or bury you here!"

Cord saw blue at the corner of his eye and saw Colonel Hatch hopping over the tongue of a wagon. When he came near, he growled, "I thought you said you could talk to them! Get 'em to make peace!"

"That was before the shooting started!" answered Cord.

"Yeah—they killed one of the settlers!" growled the colonel.

"And the settlers killed two of their warriors. Now, Broken Arrow is determined to make them leave or kill them all, and he's not particular which it takes!"

The colonel frowned, jerked his head high, and hollered, "Take cover!" pointing to the sky. Cord jerked around, looked high to see a blanket of flaming arrows arching high toward the wagons. Within seconds the storm of flames thudded to the ground, into the wagons' canvas, and at least one into the chest of a settler, whose wife screamed for help.

Several of the men had taken cover that afforded them a view of the flats to the west, but the arrows had arched overhead from beyond the rise directly to the north. As the settlers huddled behind wagons, another volley of fire arrows came from farther west of the low ridge, nearer the point, but still enough of a rise to hide the shooters. More screams accompanied the flurry of fire that fell from the sky, and a few of the men at the edges fired their rifles in the direction of the shooters, neither seeing a single warrior nor hitting one. The shooting aggravated the confusion and fear, even though it gave the shooter some satisfaction that at least he was doing something.

The colonel had organized a bucket brigade to carry water from the river and put out some of the fires. A couple wagons were too engulfed to fight and the efforts were directed at those that had yet to be consumed. Cord shouted, "Wet down the other wagons!" he turned to some of the men who were manning the spaces between the wagons, "You men! Every other one of you—go help fight the fires!" Several men came to their feet and ran to grab buckets or anything that would hold water and went to the river to join the brigade of bucket carriers.

The next flurry of arrows were without any fire and the arch of deadly darts whispered across the sky and were even more frightening as they made pincushions of the wagons and the few bodies that had not been dragged under cover. Screams, weeping, shouting, cursing, and gunfire racketed across the valley and bounced back to multiply the cacophony of fear and death that blanketed the once peaceful and sacred valley.

Colonel Hatch came alongside Cord and said, "I'm gonna mount up and give chase to them! It appears they're positioned just beyond that rise yonder," nodding to the northwest at the low point of the long ridge.

Cord answered, "That's just what they want you to do, Colonel!"

The colonel frowned, glared at Cord, "Whaddayou mean by that!" he growled, giving his best commanding officer glare to this upstart before him.

"They have two bands, Colonel. They are positioned such, that if you come after either one, the second band will quickly withdraw out of sight, and once you give chase to the fleeing band, the second will swoop down on these wagons!"

"They've got enough men here to defend against that!"

Cord shook his head, "Yeah, looks like they've been doing a bang-up job of it, too! But Colonel, if the second band doesn't come after the wagons, they will close the trap behind you, and you and your men will be caught in the open between the two bands."

"Well, we've got 'em outgunned! We can wipe 'em out in a hurry!"

"Outgunned? Colonel, they have twice the men and every one of them has a rifle and ample ammunition."

"I thought they was just shootin' arrows!"

"That's exactly what they want you to think! You might want to reconsider your action, Colonel. These people have learned battle tactics since they were hip high to their mommas!"

The colonel scowled, growled, looked around, "Hold on...looks like they've let up a mite. You think they might be leavin'?"

"Not a chance, Colonel. They won't leave until you and these wagons are gone."

"Harrumph!" growled the colonel as he stomped away to return to his men and shout some orders just to feel better about his command. He suddenly stopped, turned, and glared at Cord, "I thought you could talk 'em into peace! What happened—ain't you friends anymore?"

He started stomping back toward Cord, shaking his head and looking about. As he stood face-to-face with Cord, glowering at the man with the badge on his chest, he took several deep breaths, noticing several of the settlers watching them, and he purposely made himself calm down. He lowered his hand from his waist and lowered his voice, "So, you got any other ideas how we can stop this—maybe bring peace back?"

"I dunno, Colonel. I don't know if Broken Arrow will even talk to me. But..." he paused, shaking his head and looking around—"I'm willing to give it another try. Maybe with the lull in the shooting, I can ride out under some kind of peace flag or somethin' and he might listen. Might even help if you come along."

The colonel dropped his eyes, squirming and twisting as he looked around at the settlers, some fighting fires on the wagons, others hustling about with bandages and all showing fear on their faces and in their eyes. Even some of the soldiers, most busy helping the settlers, but some looking about with a blend of confusion and fear showing on their wide-eyed faces. Colonel Hatch turned back to Cord, "Yeah—let's give it a try. You round up some kinda flag or somethin', I'll get a pole from the company guidon, and get my horse." Without waiting for Cord's agreement, the colonel turned away and stomped off, assuming his *orders* would be carried out by the marshal.

Cord looked to the settlers, saw a group gathered about the two wagon masters, and he approached to see several men and women, including the buxom big woman, the mother of the young man who fired the first shot and was killed. Whitcomb and Martinez turned and simultaneously asked, "What'd the colonel say?"

"He agreed that we should make another attempt at stopping this fighting. We're going to go try to talk to the Ute, maybe get some agreement or..." he shrugged. "But I need some kind of flag, banner or something that will get their attention. Preferably something white." The people looked at one another, and Cord noticed the only one that moved was the big woman who turned her back and was fidgeting with something. She bent over, stood up, and turned around, "How's about this!" she declared, trying to keep a straight face. She was holding the biggest pair of white silk women's drawers with lace on the legs that Cord had ever seen, not that he had seen many, but they were bigger than a feed bag! He flinched as she threw them to him, but he caught them as she said, "That'll git thar attention! An' if they knows what they be, by the time they quit laughin' or jawin' 'bout 'em, you'll be close 'nuff to start talkin' or shootin'!"

The crowd could not help but laugh at the sight and the comment, nor could Cord. And just in time, the colonel arrived, leading his horse and carrying the pole or staff for the guidon. Cord turned and handed him the bundle of women's drawers, "I got 'em, you tie 'em on the guidon. I'm gonna get my horse!" and walked away.

29

PARLEY

"YOU HEAR THAT?" ASKED ALBERT BROWN, SCOWLING AS he looked at John Reynolds, the leader of what was now called the Wallace gang.

The leader frowned, "Sounds like gunfire. And it's a long way off, but there's lots of it."

"Whatchu reckon it is?"

"Might be Indians attacking those wagons we been followin'."

Brown frowned, thinking and listening, "Mebbe they'll kill off the fightin' men, leave the wagons and the money for us! Them injuns ain't got no use for gold or money, do they?"

"Depends on the Indians. Some might, but usually all they want are the scalps and horses. Sometimes they take the women captive, sometimes they just kill 'em all!"

The seven men were riding down the last of the trail that sided the San Juan River and would take them from the high country of the San Juan Mountains. They had been on the trail of the wagons in hopes of striking them without warning and stealing any valuables they might have and maybe find some women. This group was totally without scruples and thought only of enriching themselves in the quickest and easiest way. Along the way, they had killed and robbed every prospector that had a claim or anything that looked to be of value, but so far, their takings were minimal, and the leader, John Reynolds, who referred to himself as Wallace, was losing his patience with this journey and these men.

He looked about and motioned to a clearing on the far side of the river, just before the confluence with another stream that came from the high country to the east. The clearing lay below a timber-covered shoulder and was surrounded by juniper, cottonwood, and a smattering of aspen. He told the others, "We'll make camp there," and nudged his mount toward the river's edge. Brown asked, "Ain't it a mite early to be makin' camp?"

"That gunfire we heard could be a big fight between the settlers and the Indians. I don't want to ride up on it and find ourselves surrounded by a bunch of scalp-huntin' redskins! Now, if you wanna donate your scalp to the cause, you just go right ahead. I'm gonna get some food and rest 'fore I go down there."

CORD SHIED away when the colonel offered the guidon with the drawers, turned his back, and swung aboard Kwitcher. When the colonel led his mount close, then turned to hand the guidon to Cord, the marshal begrudgingly accepted the somewhat immodest banner, chuckling as he lifted it and placed the end of the guidon staff into his stirrup beside his boot. The two men rode side by side as the settlers pulled aside the wagon tongue and two barrels to let them pass through the makeshift barrier.

It was a little over a hundred yards to the long, low hill that had offered protection when chosen for a campsite by the wagon master, Whitcomb, but now offered a launching ramp for the barrage of fire arrows of the Ute warriors. There were random chokecherry and service berry bushes amongst the taller juniper and occasional spruce. But the covering on the hillside was not dense and easily offered a view of anyone atop or for those that waited, a view of anyone crossing the flats between the wagons and the hillside.

Cord and the colonel had just left the wagons when they saw two mounted warriors crest the hill, stop, and sit stoically as they watched the approach of the two men from the wagon trains. Cord spoke softly as he cautioned the colonel to let him to the talking and especially to not make any threats against the Ute. "They don't bluff, and they don't take threats as anything but an insult. They won't wait for you to carry out a threat, they'll just kill you on the spot," he cautioned. The colonel nodded, and as they drew closer, both men saw two other mounted warriors had crested the hill and sat beside the first two. Cord recognized the newcomers as Broken Arrow and Lone Eagle. He spoke to the colonel, "The warrior on the dapple grey is Broken Arrow, he's the leader of the Wolfpack. The other one is a woman, but she is an equal warrior to the others, and she is also the shaman or medicine woman of the people. She is the sister of Broken Arrow, her name is Lone Eagle."

As they started up the hill, it was necessary to move among the trees and brush to make their way up, and every move was watched by the Ute. As they neared the crest, Cord nodded to Broken Arrow and to Lone Eagle, who suppressed a smile as she nodded to Cord. When they neared one another, Cord greeted Broken Arrow with, *Maykwa tügwüvüchin, Hello friend,* and was answered with a nod and *Chihkachün sürüpüv, my brother.*

Cord asked, "May we talk peace?"

Broken Arrow nodded, glanced to the *peace flag,* "Is that what that is for?" and tried to stifle a grin, but failed.

Cord also grinned, "We needed something that caught your attention."

Lone Eagle laughed, "We know what those are, and it is hard not to be offended," but she was grinning as she stifled a giggle.

Cord dropped the guidon staff, jammed the pointed end into the dirt, and rested his forearms on the pommel of his saddle. He nodded to the colonel and said, "You remember the colonel?" and at Broken Arrow's nod, Cord turned toward Lone Eagle and continued, "Colonel, this is Lone Eagle, the shaman of the Uncompahgre Ute people under Chief Ouray."

The colonel held his stoic expression, nodded to Lone Eagle, and looked back to Broken Arrow. He began, "Broken Arrow, the young man who fired the first shot was foolish and went against my orders and those of the wagon master, not to mention his mother," he grinned as he pointed to the guidon banner, "Those are her drawers by the way." He gave a quick glance to Cord and knowing he was speaking contrary to what they had agreed, he continued anyway, "I know we agreed to leave, but it takes time to get that many people on the move. Now they know we must leave, and they are willing to do whatever you ask, just so they can leave in peace." He paused, looking from Broken Arrow to Lone Eagle and back to Cord.

Broken Arrow scowled and growled, "Now you say you want peace and that you will leave, but how do we know this is any different than before. We lost two of our warriors, and the Warriors of the Wolf want what you call vengeance. There are more warriors on their way here, and they want to destroy all that are before us. Most say we cannot believe what you promise, and yet you are here to make more promises that you will not keep."

The colonel shook his head and looked to Cord, yielding the talks to him with a nod. Cord spoke up, "Broken Arrow, as the colonel said, what started everything was the one young man that fired the first shot, even though he had been told not to, still he was young and foolish. We cannot let the wrong of one young man cause the death of so many! Yes, you have other warriors coming and yes there will be enough to destroy everyone down there, but you will also lose many warriors. Those people are well entrenched, and the soldiers really did not do any fighting. They were busy with the fires. But..." he glanced to the colonel—"if this continues, they will do what they have been trained to do and what they did throughout the war between the North and the South called the Civil War, and they will kill many of your warriors! And for what? Because we are not willing to try one more time to get these people out of your land? Surely you don't want that!" Cord paused, looking from Broken Arrow to Lone Eagle and dropped his eyes to the ground, then raised them to look at Broken Arrow. "We are brothers, we should settle this now and have peace."

Broken Arrow looked from Cord to the colonel and then to Lone Eagle. Cord could see the look that passed between them and knew that Lone Eagle was wanting him to agree to peace. Broken Arrow looked back at Cord, lifted his eyes to the sky, and looked back, "The sun is high. By this time tomorrow, if this valley is not empty of wagons and soldiers, we will empty it with blood and fire before sundown." He jerked the head of his mount around and rode away with nothing more than a nod to the other warriors and his sister, Lone Eagle, who glanced toward Cord, lowered her eyes, and followed Broken Arrow.

Cord looked at the colonel, grabbed the staff of the guidon, and said, "There you have it, Colonel. We best get those people moving or there's going to be a bloody slaughter the likes of which this country has never seen!" The colonel just nodded and swung his big horse around and sided Cord as they rode down the slope of the hillside to return to the wagons and deliver the message.

30

CHANGE

WHEN THE TWO MEN NEARED THE WAGONS, THEY WERE besieged with questions, "What'd they say? Can we stay? Are they gonna attack?" and more, but the questions were stayed with the uplifted hand of the colonel as he firmly spoke, "Where's the wagon masters? We need to talk and we need to do it now!" he growled as he and Cord swung down from their saddles and stood beside their mounts.

"They're bein' fetched, Colonel, but you can tell us, what're we gonna do?" asked one of the men the colonel recognized as a man that had been a bit of a leader among the people, or more of a spokesman. He had a head of thick, wavy red hair and a complexion to match. He had also scouted for the wagons and was close to the wagon master, Whitcomb.

Colonel Hatch looked around at the gathered settlers, "Folks, we've got to leave and we've got to do it in a hurry. They've given us until noon tomorrow to be gone—that means every wagon, horse, and person needs to be gone from this valley by high noon tomorrow!"

Complaints and arguments came in a flurry as many voiced their objections, gripes, and excuses, but once again the colonel stayed their response with uplifted hands. "Now listen and listen close! I can't make any of you do anything, all I can do is tell you what will happen. Those Indians are madder'n an old bear with his paw in a trap! Most of 'em want to kill y'all and do it quick! But their leader, Broken Arrow, gave us until high noon!"

"An' what if we decide we're gonna stay?!" shouted one man, he was the flaming redhead that had made himself heard before, and Cord's experience with those of that mark usually had a considerable temper. But this man seemed to be well in control and appeared to be asking the question for the others and not just himself. He was not the same one had been making threats and arguments.

The colonel scowled at the man, "If I had my way, I'd just shoot you to shut you up and let the rest of these good folks make up their own mind. But..." he looked at the others, took a deep breath to calm himself, and said, "What that chief or whatever he is, said was, if this valley ain't empty by high noon, that they would empty it with blood and fire by nightfall! Now, you willing to paint that river yonder with your blood and the blood of your woman and kids, Cyrus?"

The loud talker had quieted down as the others glared at him, and he heard the mumbles of others telling him to be quiet. The colonel looked around at the rest of the crowd, "Any other questions?" But before any could answer, the crowd parted to let the two leaders, Whitcomb and Martinez, through, to stand before the colonel.

Whitcomb asked, "I heard part of it, that they want us outta here by noon. Is that right, Colonel?"

"That's correct, sir, and I suggest you folks get started."

Whitcomb looked from the colonel to the other leader, Martinez, beside him, and asked, "But where will we go, Colonel?"

The colonel just pointed to the west and said, "Thataway! Just get outta this valley!"

"But Colonel, isn't that way still in the land of the Utes? Didn't I hear somebody say,"—he looked around for Marshal Beckett—"him, wasn't it? That said the land from the mountains to the western border of the Colorado Territory was promised to the Utes?"

Cord stepped forward and nodded, "That's right. The treaty said, 'All the land from the crest of the mountains west, from the White and Yampa Rivers in the north, and the New Mexico border in the south to the territorial border in the west.'"

The colonel looked at Cord, "So, you're sayin'

that even if they leave and head west, they'll still be in the land of the Ute people until they get out of Colorado Territory?"

"That's right, Colonel. Now, I don't know what Broken Arrow will do if you go that way, but I also know they are of the Uncompahgre or Muache Ute people, and those further west are Capotas and Weminuches, and they might even be *more* disagreeable. Really, I think the best way is to go back east. There's land all along the front range of the Rockies and more to the north. But it's your call."

"I'm tired of all this nonsense, but I ain't ready to mount an all-out war with blood thirsty Indians, not after bein' ordered to keep 'em all apart. So..." he looked at the wagon masters and said, "Back the way you came! Martinez, if you want to go back south, do it. But if you want to come with us and Whitcomb's wagons, so be it. But whatever is decided, do it now and get busy packin' and hitchin' up. I'd like to see us back in the mountains 'fore dark!"

Cord watched as several glowered at him as if it was his fault, many mumbled and complained, but all set about the work before them. No one wanted to leave a loved one behind in a puddle of blood even if it meant crossing the mountains again. He walked away from the wagons and the people, crossed the shallows of the river and rode west in the shadows of the tall timber that fell from the crest of the big hill just south of the river, the same hill that had been the encampment of the Ute before the battle. He wanted to be out of sight and out of mind. If the people wanted to blame him, so be it, whatever it took to get them away from the Ute and out of the area to a safer place. He rode past the steep talus slope that fell from the butte, around the point, and turned back to get to high ground where he could see but not be seen.

He was pleased as he watched, often with his binoculars, as the people hustled about packing their wagons and harnessing the teams and more. He focused the field glasses to look further across the neck of the river to see the lone low ridge that masked the Ute warriors and spotted several warriors, belly down, watching the settlers readying to leave. Cord moved the binoculars to see the soldiers also helping the settlers, while a few in blue stood watch over their gear and horses. Cord was relieved to see the many people working to turn back, most frustrated and greatly disappointed, and Cord remembered what he had learned before when he had been shown the maps that detailed the boundaries of his district. But he also learned what the 1968 treaty had stated that the eastern boundary of the Ute lands was bordered by the 107° longitude and that the north and south line was actually about a mile to the west of their location, where the San Juan River bent to the south and where they now were was free land, and not a part of the treaty. But he also knew it would be impossible to explain about an invisible line across the land that showed only on a paper map somewhere in a government office in Denver. All he could do was to keep the settlers, soldiers, and Ute people separate and this was the only way he knew to accomplish that peace.

———————

ALTHOUGH IT WAS A STEADY CLIMB, it was not too challenging as the wagons stretched out and started back to the east, following the wagon road that sided the San Juan River. Once away from the cut that took them from the valley, the river and road bent back to the north and the wagons lined out, a line of wagons that stretched well over a mile long. The soldiers led the way, although half of the contingent trailed the wagons, protecting the last of the wagons and the downtrodden travelers. Cord breathed heavily as they moved out, slowly rose to his feet, took another long look at the men of Broken Arrow and saw them making camp where the wagons had been. They looked about at the fire circles, the remains of several wagons and parts of others that had been left behind in their hasty retreat, and Broken Arrow began directing the clean-up. It was obvious the warriors were not happy with the work, but did exactly what they were directed.

Cord moved back from the edge of the trees, mounted up, and started down to follow the wagons. Not just because they were traveling that way, but he was also bound to cross the mountains and make his way back to Wagon Wheel Gap to find the rest of the outlaws that had hunted him and tried to kill him. As he thought about them, he slipped the Yellow Boy Winchester from the scabbard, checked the action and loads, wiped it down some and replaced it in the scabbard, all without Kwitcher missing a step. Blue was trotting ahead as usual, and Cord sat back, looking over the countryside, enjoying the quiet and the beauty of the country.

The sun was lowering over the mountains behind them as the wagons rounded the knob of a rimrock butte on the north that showed sloping timber-covered flanks that pointed to the long valley of the San Juan River. As the wagons rounded the point, they passed the confluence of the San Juan and the east fork of the San Juan River. Unknown to them, they were watched from the trees and the camp of the Wallace gang. But they were also trailed by Cordell Beckett, the man who was ready to renew his hunt for that same gang. Cord was unsuspecting that they, the members of the Wallace gang, might be on this side of the mountains, for the last time they were seen, was at Wagon Wheel Gap, that lay beside the Rio Grande on the east side of the San Juan Mountains.

He had that rare sensation climbing up his back that told him of danger. He shivered, reined up, and looked about. Something was not right. Blue had gone into a stalking stance, a low growl coming from his throat, but Cord could see nothing. He nudged

Kwitcher to the trees, kept looking about, and seeing nothing, but wary all the same. He spotted a slight clearing and determined to make his solitary camp in the trees and wait until better light on the morrow before traveling any further. He knew he could trust his animals to be watchful and would warn him of any danger, especially the mule, the less trusting of the trio.

31

OUTLAWS

Cord had made a dry camp in the trees, using the lone needles of a nearby ponderosa to make a comfortable pad under his bedroll. But he lay awake, looking up as the stars lit their lanterns for the night and as the moon rose over the eastern mountains and made itself known as it drew shadows from hiding and stretched them across the dusky flats. Cord usually enjoyed this time of night, spending time with his Lord in prayer, but he was still uneasy. After the day's happenings and the hurried getaway, there was still something unsettling about here and now, but he could not place it. The nightbirds lifted their cry, a lonesome bullfrog called for a rendezvous from the backwater of the creek below, and a coyote stretched his head high as he howled at the moon, hopeful of an answer from a lonesome female. Blue lay at his side and did not so much as lift his head, but he did lift one eyelid, wrinkling his forehead, then closed both eyes and stretched before dropping into a somber sleep.

Cord chuckled to himself, rolled to his side, and felt his rifle for reassurance, and with one arm folded under his head, he determined to sleep. But it was not long before Blue came to his feet, his nose pointing north to the valley that stretched out under the rimrock shoulders of the foothills on the east side, and Cord quickly stood, rifle in hand. He looked where Blue was watching and saw the full moon's light that blanketed the valley below in a pale-yellow glow. There were a few small cookfires that marked the camp of the wagons, and the shadowy snake of circled wagons told of their sleeping. Blue brushed past Cord's leg and went to the edge of the trees and stopped, head lowered, ears back, and a low growl rumbling in his chest. Cord stepped beside the hound and looked closer below and saw the pale glow of the coals of a fire between the rivers just east of the confluence. There was no movement, nor any activity that told of an early cookfire. Cord thought it might be nothing but a campfire of some prospector that had left the coals for warmth as he slept.

He had a thought of Indians that might have followed the wagons or approached from another camp, but they would not be so careless as to leave a fire that would give away their presence by both the light and the smoke or smell. That had to be a camp of a White man, prospector, or someone else that might be up to no good. Cord watched the camp for a short while, shook his head, and returned to his bedroll. Blue had relaxed and followed Cord, stretching out beside his master. Cord glanced to the horse and mule and neither showed alarm—both stood hipshot and resting.

————

BEFORE FIRST LIGHT, Cord awoke but did not move. He moved only his eyes as he looked about, first to the horse and mule, but they stood unmoving, and the dog, but he too was still. He listened, but there was nothing save the gentle movement of the morning breeze that whispered through the nearby pines. The leaves of the few aspen at the edge of the clearing began their applause of the coming day, but even that was almost soundless. It seemed to be a perfect, quiet, still morning and Cord slowly came from his blankets, rifle in hand, as he stood in a crouch, searching the area around his small camp.

Seeing nothing, he admonished himself for being a *Nervous Nellie,* and picked up his Bible, the binoculars, wrapped his pistol belt and holster around his middle, and started through the trees toward a nearby rocky shoulder he had chosen the night before. As he seated himself on the dry moss-covered boulder, he stretched out toward the north. Off his right shoulder was the valley of the east fork of the San Juan, and before him lay the north fork and the valley that held the wagons. It was a brisk morning, the kind Cord liked, and he leaned back, his arms outstretched behind him for support and he lifted his eyes to the last of the morning's lanterns and began his prayer, thinking of the travelers, his friends with the Utes, and himself and the task that lay before him. When he muttered his "Amen," his eyes turned to the east up the valley and saw the beginning of the morning as the first light began to chase away the darkness.

Within moments, the eastern sky was ablaze with the brilliant colors of red, orange, and a hint of yellow, and the sunrise began to stretch bold lances into the dark sky. The fiery sunrise reminded Cord of the ancient mariners saying *Red sky at night, sailor's delight, red sky at morning, sailor's take warning.* He also knew that same thought was expressed in the Bible in Matthew 16:2-3, but the Bible referred to it as fair weather versus foul weather and continued to call the sayer of such, a hypocrite for discerning the *face of the sky; but can ye not discern the signs of the times?* Cord shook his head at the thought, but watched as those lances of red seemed to paint the bellies of the clouds that lay low in the west. Now the brilliance of the sunrise had spread a hue of red across the land, coloring even the black forests of the mountains.

Cord wanted to stay and watch the colors and enjoy the handiwork of the Creator, but he felt a kick in his rear by his guilty conscience when he was reminded of his father's quoting one of his favorite

Bible verses, Ecclesiastes 9:10, *Whatsoever thy hand findeth to do; do it with thy might; for there is no work, nor device, nor knowledge, nor wisdom, in the grave, whither thou goest.*

Cord looked at Blue, rubbed behind the dog's ears, and said, "Well, boy, I reckon we need to be gettin' a move on!" and began to rise, but he caught movement from below and dropped back down, stretching out to make less of a figure and lifted his binoculars. Below him, on the point of land at the confluence of the rivers, movement of men and horses was evident. He watched, frowning, thinking some of the horses looked familiar, and then slowly shook his head as he realized, those horses, at least three of them, had been ridden by the Wallace or Reynolds gang. He lifted his binoculars to the wagons, saw movement beginning, and then looked back at the outlaw camp. They were readying to break camp, so Cord slipped back into the trees and quickly went to his gear and began to saddle up Kwitcher and rig the mule. He snatched some jerky from his packs and chewed on the tough, dried meat as he worked, thinking about the bacon and biscuits that were on the cookfires of the settlers.

———

"Now what're we gonna do, boss?" asked Albert Brown, looking to Wallace as they watched the last of the wagons pass. The line of wagons was strung out for over a mile, and the soldiers of the Ninth Cavalry had split, half taking the lead and the other half trailing the wagons. Wallace stood watching as the men of the cavalry rode two by two in the tracks of the wagons. He was trying to count the number of soldiers, having already counted the wagons.

Wallace turned to look at his new number two, although Brown had been with him since the days of the Reynolds gang, only now had he stepped into the trusted second spot, after the killing of Blondy by the prospector at their last stop. Wallace growled, "I ain't too happy 'bout them so'jer boys, but some o' them wagons look like they might be worth takin'. We'll foller 'em a ways when they pull out tomorrow, see what the so'jers do then. If we see a chance, we just might take it."

———

COME MORNING, Wallace kicked Brown awake and motioned for him to follow. It was early, and the sun had yet to show its face, and Brown grumbled all the way as he followed Wallace. The man stopped at the edge of the camp that was on the high side of the embankment of the San Juan. There were alders and fir, a couple tall ponderosa, all lining the shoulder of the bank and offering ample cover for their surveillance of the wagons. Wallace leaned against the big ponderosa, scanned the wagons with his binoculars, and slowly grinned as he watched the camp. He mumbled, "Them so'jer boys done left! Ain't a one of 'em in sight nowhere!" he chuckled. "This's gonna be easier'n I thot!" He looked around at the others and began, "Now, this is what we're gonna do...Brown, I want you to take Barnes there, I'll keep the new ones with me, and you're gonna catch up to them wagons, but not till nightfall, less'n you get a special opportunity...and then I want'chu to..." And he detailed his plan for the two men to disable a couple wagons that appeared would be in the tail end of the train, making them a prime target for *help* from the passing strangers.

CORD STOOD at the edge of his camp, looking down on the camp of the outlaws. He was certain it was the same bunch, maybe a few new ones, that had terrorized the miners around Wagon Wheel Gap and along the Rio Grande headwaters. He had recognized the big black horse ridden by Wallace, and a blaze-face bay ridden by one of the others. A dapple grey also looked familiar, but he was uncertain about the others.

Cord lifted his binoculars to the camp of the wagons and could tell they were ready to pull out. But he did not see the boys in blue and wondered what the colonel was up to now. He looked back to the camp of the outlaws and saw they were also making ready to leave. Cord took the time to scan the valley before him, focusing on the tree lines at the edge of the valley, anticipating the need to stay in the trees if he chose to follow the outlaws, and he would, if he thought they were going to follow the wagons. The west side of the valley had long timbered slopes that fell gently from the higher mountains, while the east side with the heavy-shouldered mountains with rimrock abutments standing forbiddingly over the valley, offered little in the way of game trails but would offer better cover where he could follow unseen. But the trail of the wagons stayed on the east side of the river, and he would be able to move alongside or even get well ahead. Another look at the west side showed a tempting trail, but that would also give less cover, and any movement would be more easily noticeable, even though game would come from that type of country to water in the river.

As he watched, the wagons had started on their way toward the narrow cut that carried the trail that followed Wolf Creek into the high country. A short time later, the five mounted men came from the trees, leading a single horse with a saddle that was laden down with other gear. The converted pack horse was a dapple grey and Cord remembered that horse as the one ridden by the big man called Blondy, but now he saw no man that resembled Blondy. He shrugged, thought, *I guess he got lost along the way.* Returning to his animals, Cord swung aboard and pointed the grulla to the trail to cross the east fork of the San Juan River and take to the timber.

32

PURSUIT

THE ROUTE THAT WAS BEING CALLED WOLF CREEK PASS had long been used by the migrating Ute peoples that would travel to the better buffalo hunting in the plains during the summer and fall, and return to the mountains in the early spring. In the 1700s, French and Spanish explorers were said to have traveled this way, and it was near Treasure Falls, so a legend says, the French buried a massive treasure of raw gold. Some had also said there were several Mormons that took this route to their promised land of Zion in Utah, but there were no records of such passing. However, the trail had certainly at some time in the not-too-distant past, been used by wagons and not just the occasional two-wheel cart, but the wagons used by settlers. However, since that had not been a regular occurrence, the trail, oft called a hairline trail, hugged the east face of the steep mountains and overlooked the small Wolf

Creek in the bottom. The road was narrow and often precipitous and for all the travelers, hair-raising.

To overcome some of the potential hazards, wagon master Whitcomb conferred with the master from the Santa Fe wagons and they agreed to stagger the wagons with every other one being from Whitcomb's experienced wagon handlers. When they neared the mouth of the canyon of Wolf Creek, they stopped and the wagon masters rode back alongside the wagons to caution every driver about the road. Whitcomb spoke, "Remember men, this is not an easy pull for your teams, but we must keep moving. If it gets too hard for them, you might have to lighten the load. I know our people had to do that quite often and they have little left to throw out, but those of you from Santa Fe might have to consider your teams and lighten up a little. This would be a good time to do that. Now, once we start up, don't lag behind if you can help it. We'll keep track of everyone, and after we top out, there will be a time to rest, we might even spend the night."

"Cap'n, what'd the soldiers do—leave us?" asked one of the wives sitting on the seat with her man.

"No ma'am, they just went on ahead to clear any rocks that might have fallen, or timber, or such. They also are scouting the trail to make sure there's no wagons coming from that direction."

"What about injuns?"

The wagon master shook his head, "No tellin'

'bout them. But the soldiers are keeping a scout out for that also."

"Good, good," replied an obviously worried woman as she leaned against her husband.

When the wagon masters reached the end of the line, they agreed Whitcomb would return to the lead and Martinez would stay further back, just in case of trouble. He would move up and back as needed to help. As Whitcomb quickly rode to the front, he stopped, stood in his stirrups, and shouted back, "Waagonns—move out!" and waved them to get started. The drivers cracked whips, tossed pebbles, shouted, and more, anything to get the animals on the move. Most wagons were pulled by a team of draught horses or a four-up of lesser horses. There were a few that had a four-up of mules, but all had proved their worth in the days before.

As the animals leaned into their traces, heads down, front hooves digging deep, rear hooves moving earth, the trace chains rattled, wheels creaked, wagons groaned, and the movement began. In short order, lather was showing under the harnesses, but the cool air of the high country helped, and the animals labored consistently and without complaint. They passed Fall Creek and Trea-sure Falls, moving at a steady pace, but the real climb had yet to start. Shortly after Fall Creek, the road narrowed, laying under the heavy shoulders of the mountain on the east, then dropped down into the creek bottom to cross over on a switchback bend, that made another switchback after about a half mile to start the long, grueling climb towards the crest about six and a half miles away.

The wagons began this challenging and perilous part of the climb with the two switchbacks, although the doing of it was foreboding and time-consuming, it was a good test and eye-opener for those that had yet to travel the pass. Several stopped after the switchback for a short rest to let the horses blow before resuming the long pull to the top. Unknown to the travelers, they were being watched by two men who had been dispatched by the Wallace gang, two men who had taken the trail from below the beginning of the long haul. A trail that had its own switchbacks but climbed steadily, taking the two riders up a narrow trail that split some jagged and ragged formations that stood below the second switchback but gave the two men a way into the trees and cover that overlooked the hazardous bends.

"What're we gonna do, Al?" asked the man known as Barnes or Johnny.

Barnes was a bit of what some would call a *fancy-pants* who took a little more pride in the way he dressed and kept clean. But he was smaller than Albert Brown, who had become the number two man in the Wallace gang, even though they had both been with Wallace the same amount of time. Brown was a big man, lantern-jawed, broad-shouldered, and tall with black hair that had a white streak on the side.

Some would try to call him *Skunk* but usually to their dismay and often their death.

Brown looked at the wagons, counted five left in the long line that had yet to make the switchback, and Brown looked at Barnes, "We're gonna move over there. When that wagon with the mules rounds this bend, we're gonna stop 'em."

The road was pushed away by a massive limestone shoulder, making the bend of the road and the shoulder block the view of those wagons that had already passed. The tall spruce and aspen thicket provided the cover for the two riders as they dropped to the road between wagons. As the mule team and wagon straightened out after the switchback, they were faced by two strangers, the bigger holding up his hand to signal the wagon to stop. The driver, a man called Solomon Girty, pulled back on the leads, calling, "Whoa up mules," as he stretched out his foot to the brake lever, bringing the wagon to a stop. The driver wrapped the leads around the brake handle, snatched up his rifle, and growled at the men, "What's the matter with you! Can't you see this is a steep hill and ain't no place to be stopping!"

"Now hold on, hold on," began Brown, "Muh friend here's a wheelwright, an' he heard that creakin' and groanin' and squealin' when we was takin' the trail up top. He tol' me to stop, an' he listened and said, '*Those folks're in trouble! That wagon's gonna snap a kingpin,*' whatever that is, an' I tol' him weren't none of our bizness. But he swore we had to help you or else'n you an' the missus there would prob'ly have a turrible wreck—mebbe get kilt!" The driver seemed to relax a bit, lowered his rifle, and looked at the smaller man, Barnes.

The driver asked Barnes, "You're a wheelwright?"

"That's right. Least I was 'fore I left Independence. Worked at the Young Wagon Works. An' I could tell from what I was hearin', you got troubles. Better let me take a look!" stated Barnes, starting to swing down from his saddle. The driver, Solomon, watched as the man came near, put his hand on the edge of the box, and leaned down to look at the undercarriage of the wagon. He muttered, "Ummhmm," and looked at Girty and said, "I'm gonna crawl under there to take a better look. Don't move the wagon else you'll run me over!"

"Oh, no, I won't," answered Solomon Girty with a concerned glance to his wife. He lay his rifle across his legs and leaned over to see the boots of Barnes sticking out from under the wagon. Suddenly, several thuds and bangs from underneath told of the man doing something, and then Barnes crawled out, held up a long metal rod, and said, "Just as I thought. You're kingpin is gettin' weak,"—and pointed to a worn spot—"see there—it's about to break off. An' if that'd happened on that grade, you'da gone right o'er the side!"

"Well, what can we do?" asked Solomon, "I don't have another one."

"Well, mebbe them folks behind you do," offered

Barnes, keeping the attention on himself and the pin he held.

While he spoke, Brown had ridden close, looking behind the wagon and lifting his hand as if stopping the others. But when he was close to the driver's box, he slipped out his pistol and shot Girty in the back of the head, turned the pistol on the wife, who started to scream, and shot her through the neck.

He growled at Barnes, "Get that strongbox!" pointing at the feet of the slumped-over driver. "I'm goin' back to the next wagon 'fore they get antsy!"

WHEN CORD DETERMINED to see what the outlaw gang was up to, it did not take long to know they were planning on something for the wagons. Cord left his camp, took to the trees, and a high game trail that would take him under the shadow of the rocky bluffs on the east side of the valley of the San Juan River. He also knew from Broken Arrow, that this trail would take him into Fall Creek and afford him a way over the top that would overlook the valley of Wolf Creek and the trail over the pass.

Concerned about whatever the gang was planning, Cord wanted to get to the head of the line and give warning, but he also wanted a promontory so that he could see most of the wagons as they traversed the eyebrow trail on the precipitous edge of the mountains. He did not want to presume on what

Wallace would plan, knowing he had shown himself a crafty planner and one that did not take too many chances, but he also believed the man was getting a little more anxious and maybe desperate, so he might try just about anything. As Cord kept Kwitcher to the trail that started over the ridge, it was a considerable climb and wove in and out through the trees.

He began to try to think like an outlaw and what he would do if he was going to attack some wagons. His first thought was it would be foolish to attack so many wagons with both soldiers and fighting men that were experienced on the trail. But Wallace was desperate for money, and he believed some of the wagons might be easy pickings if he could separate a few from the others, but how?

Cord crested the ridge, pulled up in the shadow of a tall spruce, and lifted his binoculars. He could see the wagon trail that bent around the point just past Treasure Falls, and there were still about eight or ten wagons that were at the tail end of the train and were moving slowly along the trail. He could see the difficult switchbacks as the trail crossed Wolf Creek and knew the wagons would have to take it slow and easy. As he watched, he thought this would be a good place to get at the stragglers, and he realized that was probably what Wallace had planned. Cord slapped legs to the big grulla, pulling the lead of the mule taut and sending Blue scampering down the trail ahead of them.

He had a ways to go, but the experienced trail horse and mule knew what was expected and they cut through the timber, never missing a step as they took to the trail that traversed the flat top butte and pointed them toward the drop off by Lake Creek, but Cord grew anxious and turned them toward the bluff above Wolf Creek that might afford a shooting position if needed.

But a long draw fell steeply before them, and the big horse dropped his haunches and began the long slide. With forelegs extended and Cord leaning so far back, his shoulders rubbed the haunches of the grulla, the horse slid on his back hooves, stepping with his front. Cord had let loose the lead for the mule, but the long-eared galoot stayed right with them and was mimicking the horse as the animals slid their way to the bottom. As they neared the bottom, Cord dared a look at the wagon road and saw nothing. No wagons from this point back down the slope to the mouth of Wolf Creek, but the rocking bonnets of the other wagons continued on their way, apparently oblivious to the stragglers.

When they bottomed out, Cord stepped down, letting the horse and mule and even Blue slake their thirst after that dusty slide. Cord tiptoed, stepped atop a nearby boulder, looking down the creek to the trail that rode the talus slope on the north side. He spotted what appeared to be wagons down nearer the switchbacks, and then he heard a gunshot, and another. He leaped spread-legged from the boulder into his saddle, slapped legs to the grulla as he drove his boots into the stirrups and grabbed for the rifle in the scabbard. He brought it up before him, nudged the grulla to take to the slope below the road and quickly crested the roadway. Before him was the bulge of rock that had pushed the road around the point, and Cord dropped to the ground, quickly taking to the edge and looking around the point.

He spotted the two horses with one man on the ground, the other starting back toward the other wagons at the tail end of the line. The smaller man beside the wagon started to mount up and follow the first man, but Cord had jacked a round in the chamber and lifted his rifle for a quick shot that emptied the saddle as the bloodied Barnes fell face down in the dirt. Cord ran toward the blaze-faced bay horse that stood trembling beside the body of his rider, and Cord grabbed the reins, ducked under the neck, and with his left hand on the reins at the bit, the rifle in his right, and using the horse as a shield, Cord moved almost in the shadow of the first man toward the next wagon.

Brown frowned as he saw Barnes' horse come from beside the wagon and called out, "You all right? What was that shootin'?"

Cord coughed, kept moving, and answered in a raspy voice, "That'n back 'ere moved, so I shot him agin!"

Brown frowned, leaned to the side to get a better look at who he thought was Barnes, but Cord saw him lean and lifted his Winchester and let loose a messenger of death that entered Brown's chest in front of his right arm and exited behind his left, taking every vital organ for life with it. Brown's eyes flared, his face winced with hatred, but the shock of the bullet made the big man slump over the neck of his horse and he unknowingly dug heels into the sides of the blood sorrel that he had taken from the dead Dixie, and the horse leaped forward to start down the trail as Brown slid from the saddle.

Another gunshot sounded, and Cord looked down the trail toward the two other wagons and saw what could only be more of the gang. Four other riders that Cord assumed were the rest of the Wallace gang, had come from behind and were confronting the last of the wagons, each wagon with a man on either side, holding guns on the drivers and making their demands. Cord shook his head, knowing they did not realize what had happened to the first two men that stopped the first wagon. Cord grabbed the reins of the bay, stepped aboard, and hunched over to partially conceal his appearance and started toward the other wagons.

As he neared, one man called out, "Hey Barnes! Get o'er here an' help with this wagon!"

Cord reined the bay that way, saw one of the men still pointing a pistol at the frightened driver and his woman, both with hands raised and blubbering some kind of plea for mercy. Cord swung the muzzle of his Winchester toward that outlaw and fired again. The bullet taking the man high in the chest at the base of his throat. The man started falling backwards but squeezed the trigger of his pistol, and fortunately the bullet went high.

The man who hollered for Barnes turned to look at his first partner, back to Barnes, but realized that was not Barnes, as he was staring down the muzzle of a smoking Winchester that was held by a glaring stranger. "Drop it!" ordered Cord, waving the muzzle at the man to make his point. The outlaw, one of the new men in the gang, instantly dropped his pistol and lifted his hands. Cord looked at the driver, "Get his pistol, and if you have something to tie him up, do it!"

"Yessir! You betcha! Thank you, sir!" declared the man, his relief obvious as he started to step down, but leaned around the edge of the canopy of his wagon and turned back to look back at Cord, "What about them?" he pointed to the wagon behind him.

Cord asked, "How many are there?"

The man craned around to look again, "Looks like two—just like these were!"

Cord nodded, motioned to the driver to get the outlaw on the ground, and stepped to the ground himself. He quickly moved to the side of the wagon and worked his way to the rear. He saw the two other men, one with a pistol pointed at the driver and his woman, the other man on the ground with a rifle. The man on the ground was reaching for the rope that tied the cover of the wagon down to start stripping it back, probably to try to find any valuables. The outlaws had no reason to be concerned about their cohorts, probably believing the gunshots were aimed at the settlers. Cord saw there was no cover for him to try to approach down the road, but a quick glance to both sides only offered some brush on the uphill side, and the edge of the road on the downhill side.

He was only about fifty to sixty feet away, and he leaned a shoulder on the tailgate edge of the wagon beside him, took a leaning stance, and called out, "Drop it or die! This is Marshal Beckett!"

But the mounted man just turned and cut loose with his pistol, firing rapidly as he lay low on the neck of his horse that he had turned toward Cord and kicked hard in the ribs to charge directly at Cord. At the same time, the man on the ground turned and fired his rifle as Cord ducked and dropped to the ground beside the hind wheel. But Cord was not to be buffaloed and took a quick but careful aim and fired at the charging rider, who he realized was Wallace himself, the bullet passing just past the head of the horse and plowing a deep crease across the back of the rider. The wound was painful and surprising, and Wallace sat up, screaming, just in time to take another shot from Cord's rifle. The horse swerved quickly to miss the wagon and stumbled over the edge of the road, rolling and kicking over the rider, repeatedly rolling over the man, and probably kicking him in the process.

But Cord was more concerned with the second shooter who had dropped to the ground behind the team of horses, then rose and slapped the flat of the rifle stock on the rump of one horse who lunged in his traces, startling the driver that had locked the brake lever, and now grabbed up the lead lines, pulling back as hard as he could and shouting, "Whoa horses, whoa!" but the outlaw fired a shot under the team at Cord, startling the animals that spooked, fought, kicked, and screamed their whinnies.

Cord was looking for a shot at the outlaw, but the crazed animals prevented him taking a shot, not wanting to make the team fight even more. Cord rolled under the nearby wagon, came up on the side near the face of the hill, looked quickly toward the shooter but saw that man was also trying to get a shot but was prevented by the panicking horses. Cord lunged for the hillside, clawed up the face of the slope, and took cover behind a tree trunk. He worked around the big ponderosa trunk and spotted the shooter, and it was easy to see he had not seen Cord's escape. Cord grinned, lifted his Winchester, and took aim, but did not shoot. Instead, he stood and started walking across the side slope toward the shooter. As he neared, he called out, "Drop it or eat lead!"

The man quickly turned, but spotted Cord and saw he was in the marshal's sights, and dropped his rifle and lifted his hands high, shouting, "Don't shoot! Don't shoot!"

"On your belly—now!" shouted Cord, as he continued slow steps toward the man. He watched as the outlaw dropped on his belly, and Cord came close, stood behind the man, and motioned the driver of the wagon over. As the driver neared, Cord reached in his hind pocket and grabbed the manacles and tossed them to the driver, "Put those on him!" and watched as the driver did as bidden.

33

TRIAL

THE GUNFIRE AND THE ACCOMPANYING RUCKUS HAD attracted the attention of the other wagons, even though they had continued on the move. However, the word quickly spread to the wagon master and others that were riding alongside, and it was only a short while before several men came riding back down the line, each with rifles or pistols at the ready. They slowed up at the bend, and Whitcomb asked one of the others, "Isn't that the marshal's horse and mule?"

The closest rider, a man called Caleb, answered, "Believe it is, Cap'n," and another man agreed.

Whitcomb motioned them to follow closely as they rounded the point and spotted the first wagon. As they neared the closest wagon, they spotted the dead bodies, and the leader, Whitcomb, raised his hand to stop the men and looked at the others, "Alright, men, get ready. There's somethin' bad happenin' here and its your guess as good as mine. I don't think it's Indians, though." He gave a wave with his rifle and led the way cautiously past the wagon, glancing only briefly at the bodies of the man and woman still on the seat of the wagon, blood all about. It was evident they were dead, and Whitcomb kept moving.

One of the other men, the redhead, had chosen to move on the outside of the wagon while Whitcomb led several along the inside, keeping between the steep slope and the road. The redhead had three men following as they carefully rode past the wagon on the precipitous edge of the road that overlooked the creek in the bottom. As they passed the wagon, they could see movement beside the next wagon, and a familiar man stood and waved as they neared. "Cap'n,"—referring to the wagon master with the familiar term—"I shore am glad to see you men, but I think the shootin's over! The marshal came a runnin' and a gunnin' and I think he got 'em all! This'n here's tied up and gagged, I got tired o'listenin' to him whine."

"How many were there?" asked Whitcomb, glancing about at the others but keeping a look down trail.

"Dunno, I think they was two per wagon, one on each side. Leastways that's what they done to us, an' I think that's what happened with them folks," he explained, nodding back up to the first wagon attacked.

Whitcomb motioned to the others, "Easy does it, men. We don't know what we're gettin' into!" He nudged his mount forward, and the others followed close beside and behind him. As they neared the second wagon, the driver and his woman were standing beside it, looking back toward the last wagon and looked at the approaching men, familiar faces all.

"Benjamin, you an' the missus alright?"

"Yessir, we are. Not too sure 'bout them folks back there. Been a lotta shootin' but it seems to have stopped now."

Whitcomb and his men continued past the second wagon and slowly approached the last wagon. Several horses stood about, and the marshal stepped from behind the wagon, "Howdy!" he called, relief showing on his face. He waited for Whitcomb to come close and watched as the wagon master stepped down.

Whitcomb asked, a bit incredulously, "What happened?"

Cord simply answered, "An outlaw gang led by a fella name of Reynolds. He went by the name of Wallace, and I know the names of a couple the others, but some I just don't know."

"What..." Whitcomb shrugged, looking from Cord to the bodies and the other men and back to Cord.

"Well, I spotted them back at the forks. They were camped on the point of land at the forks and watched as the wagons rolled past. I think they were planning something from the first time they saw you. I was on the hill above them, saw them watching you but wasn't too sure who they were, although I suspected. So, when they pulled out after you, I circled around to get in front of 'em and they hit the wagons sooner'n I expected. But...there were six of 'em, four are dead, two are captured." While Cord spoke, most of the other men also dismounted and came closer to hear the story of the attack.

"I never expected something like this, especially when we had the cavalry with us."

"Ummhmm, but they saw the cavalry leave. I think that's what made 'em think they could get away with it. I don't know what they did to stop the first wagon up there, but you can see they waited till the others were around that point before they came out." Cord paused and pointed to the bluff across the creek, "I came across over there, down that draw just past that butte, but didn't get here in time to stop the first killin'." Cord took a deep breath and turned back to the men.

Whitcomb asked, "What're you gonna do with those two?"

"Prob'ly hafta take 'em to Canon City, that's where the only court that I know is located."

"But that's, what, a week's ride away?"

"'Bout that," answered Cord.

One of the other men, the redhead, stepped forward, "Maybe not, Marshal. Let me introduce myself. My name is James Belford. I'm the associate judge for this district, so if you want to turn them over to us, we can hold court at the next stop and settle the issue here. That way, you won't have to make that trip, unless we decide to sentence them to prison, then..." he shrugged.

Cord stepped back, looked at the man, and remembered him being called, *The red-headed rooster of the Rockies,* and Cord grinned. "Well, I must admit, I was not expecting that. But you're the judge, so whatever you say suits me just fine!"

"That all right with you, Mr. Whitcomb?" asked the judge.

"Certainly! We'll get things together here, try to catch back up with the others, and if we stop up top for the night, we can have court there." At the nod of the judge, Whitcomb turned to the others, "Caleb, you and Ebson there, put the bodies of those in the first wagon in the wagon, and Caleb, you drive and see if you can catch up with the others."

Caleb nodded, and he and Ebson walked together, leading their horses back up the trail to the first wagon. Ebson frowned as he looked beside the dead body of the one outlaw, bent down to pick up the kingpin, and said, "Uh, don't move that yet!" pointing to the wagon. "We need to put this back in place," as he held up the kingpin. "I bet this is what got 'em to stop the wagons."

The rest of the men stepped to the task of picking up the dead bodies. They had agreed to take them to the top where the other wagons would stop and they would be buried there. Cord thought it was a waste of time and energy, thinking it would be easier to cave in part of the embankment over the bodies and call it good, but he was overruled by the wagon master and the others.

They were soon on their way back up the trail, and Cord followed a good distance behind, wanting to give Kwitcher an easy go after the downhill slide. Cord had checked out the hind hocks, and both the horse and mule had lost a little hair but otherwise were in good shape. Now he just wanted to take it easy, and as he rode along, he thought about the people, the fight with the outlaws, and the presence of the judge, and could not help but take a few moments to mutter a prayer of thanksgiving to his Lord for keeping him safe.

One of the men had erected a desk and chair atop and makeshift platform that gave the judge a place above the others for him to hold court. He had appointed a man to be the defense attorney and asked Cord to serve as the prosecutor. "I know that's a little irregular, but since you were there, you know more about what happened. And you're a trust-worthy sort, aren't you?" he asked, grinning.

Cord chuckled, shook his head slightly, and looked over at the two men who sat, hands bound behind their backs. With a drop of the gavel, the court session began and did a quick job of having the evidence presented by the witnesses in the second and third wagons and by Cord. The two men were allowed to talk, and only one chose to address the court. "Uh, your honor, judge, I ain't been with these fellas long 'nuff to do much. I din't like the idee o'going against this hyar wagon train, but the others did, so..." he shrugged, looking at the other man who snarled at him and glared as he tried to kick at him. The talker stepped away, looked back at the judge, "So, if you'll let me off, I promise I won't never do nuthin' like this agin. I'll even leave the country if you say so!"

The judge stared stoically at the man and waited until he seated himself, then explained in a calm manner, "The law tells us that anyone that is a part of a group of two or more, and the group murders another, then everyone that was a part of that group and present at the committing of that crime, is equally guilty." He turned his attention to the group of men that were standing at the side and addressed them, "You men have been chosen as the jury. You have heard the testimony, and now you must make a decision as to the guilt of these two men. Do you need to retire to another location and confer in quiet?"

The men looked around at one another, and one of the men that stood at the front, after looking at each one as they conferred together in hushed tones, nodded, turned back to the judge and pronounced, "No, sir, Mr. Judge, we don't need to confer. We done decided. They be guilty and oughta hang!"

"So be it!" declared the judge, dropping his gavel like a hammer to the tabletop. He looked at the men, "I hereby sentence you to be hanged by the neck until dead!" The judge then looked at the two wagon masters and asked, "Are you prepared to help carry out the sentence?"

The two leaders looked at one another, nodded, and back to the judge, and Whitcomb answered, "We are, Your Honor. And we've already selected a tree!"

"Then carry out the sentence forthwith!" and again dropped the gavel.

———

CORD WAS SOMBER as he turned away and went to his tethered animals. He stroked the face of Kwitcher and asked quietly, "How 'bout we just leave these folks behind, huh, fella?" He chuckled to himself, realizing he had momentarily expected his faithful mount to at least shake his head. But he grinned, tightened the latigo, grabbed the lead of the mule, and swung aboard Kwitcher. With a wave of his hand to Blue, the trio of friends took to the trail, choosing to leave the wagons and the people to their own doings. He rode past the encampment of the soldiers, nodded to the colonel as he passed, and with his back to the setting sun, he started the last leg of his trek back to Wagon Wheel Gap.

A LOOK AT: ANIMAS FORKS
(THE QUEST CHRONICLES 8)

DUTY. DESPERATION. LAWLESS ACTION.

Colorado Territory simmers with unrest, and Deputy Marshal Cordell Beckett stands in the fire. As the Ute push for a new treaty and gold camps spread like wildfire, the Buffalo Soldiers are sent west with orders that seemed impossible. Cord must navigate fragile negotiations, track claim jumpers through unforgiving terrain, and face down a ruthless band of vaqueros driving stolen cattle straight into the heart of the Rockies.

Cord's badge still means something—but it won't stop the bullets or ease the burden. Every ride into the high country leaves him more worn, more alone, and more certain that the life he dreams of—a ranch, a family, peace—is slipping further out of reach.

In a land where greed knows no borders and justice rides alone, can one lawman hold the line?

ABOUT THE AUTHOR

Born and raised in Colorado into a family of ranchers and cowboys, B.N. Rundell is the youngest of seven sons. Juggling bull riding, skiing, and high school, graduation was a launching pad for a hitch in the Army Paratroopers. After the army, he finished his college education in Springfield, MO, and together with his wife and growing family, entered the ministry as a Baptist preacher.

With many years as a successful pastor and educator, he retired from the ministry and followed in the footsteps of his entrepreneurial father and started a successful insurance agency, which is now in the hands of his trusted nephew. Having finally realized his life-long dream, B.N. has turned his efforts to writing a variety of books, from children's picture books and young adult adventure books, to the historical fiction and Western genres, which are his first loves.